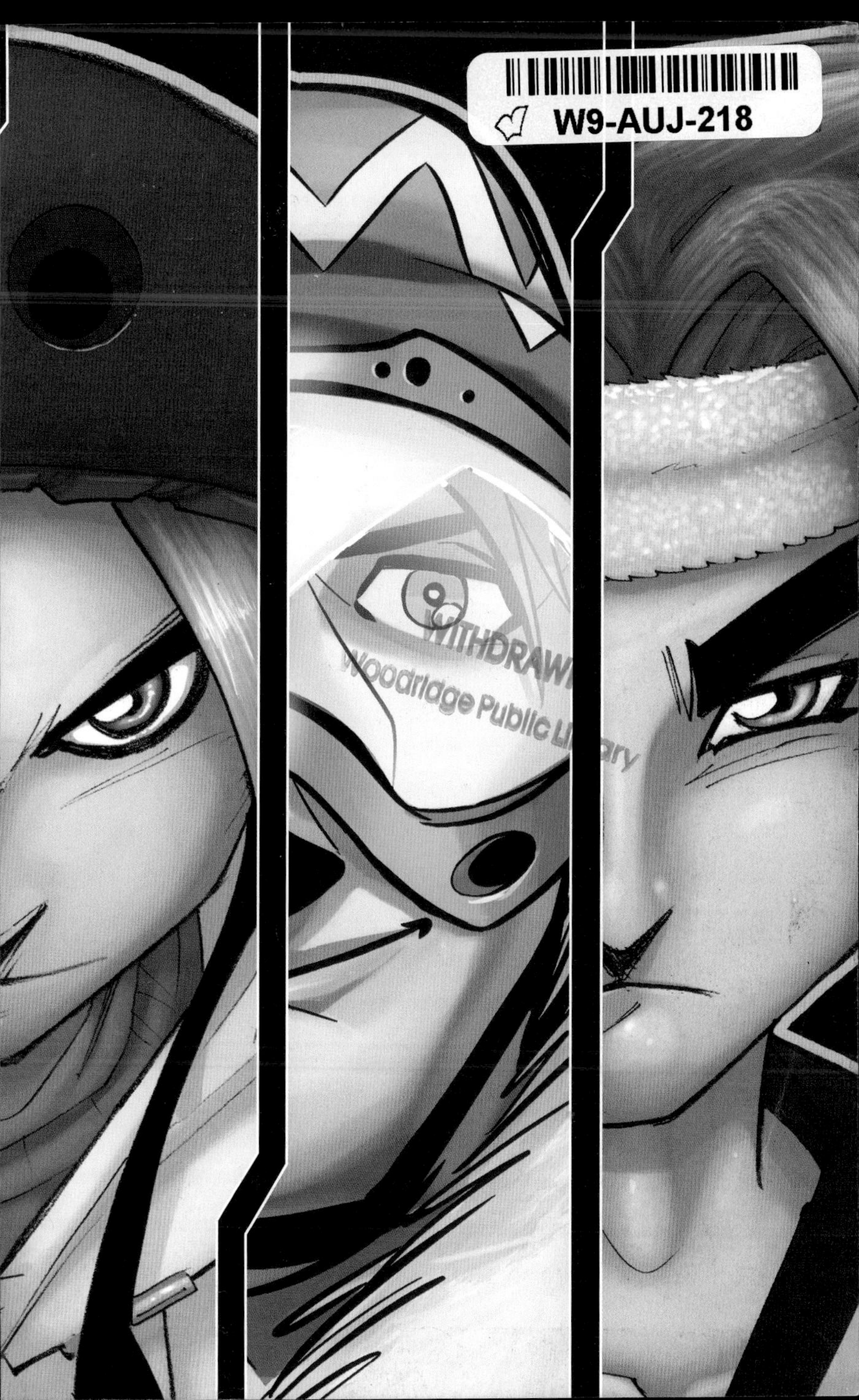

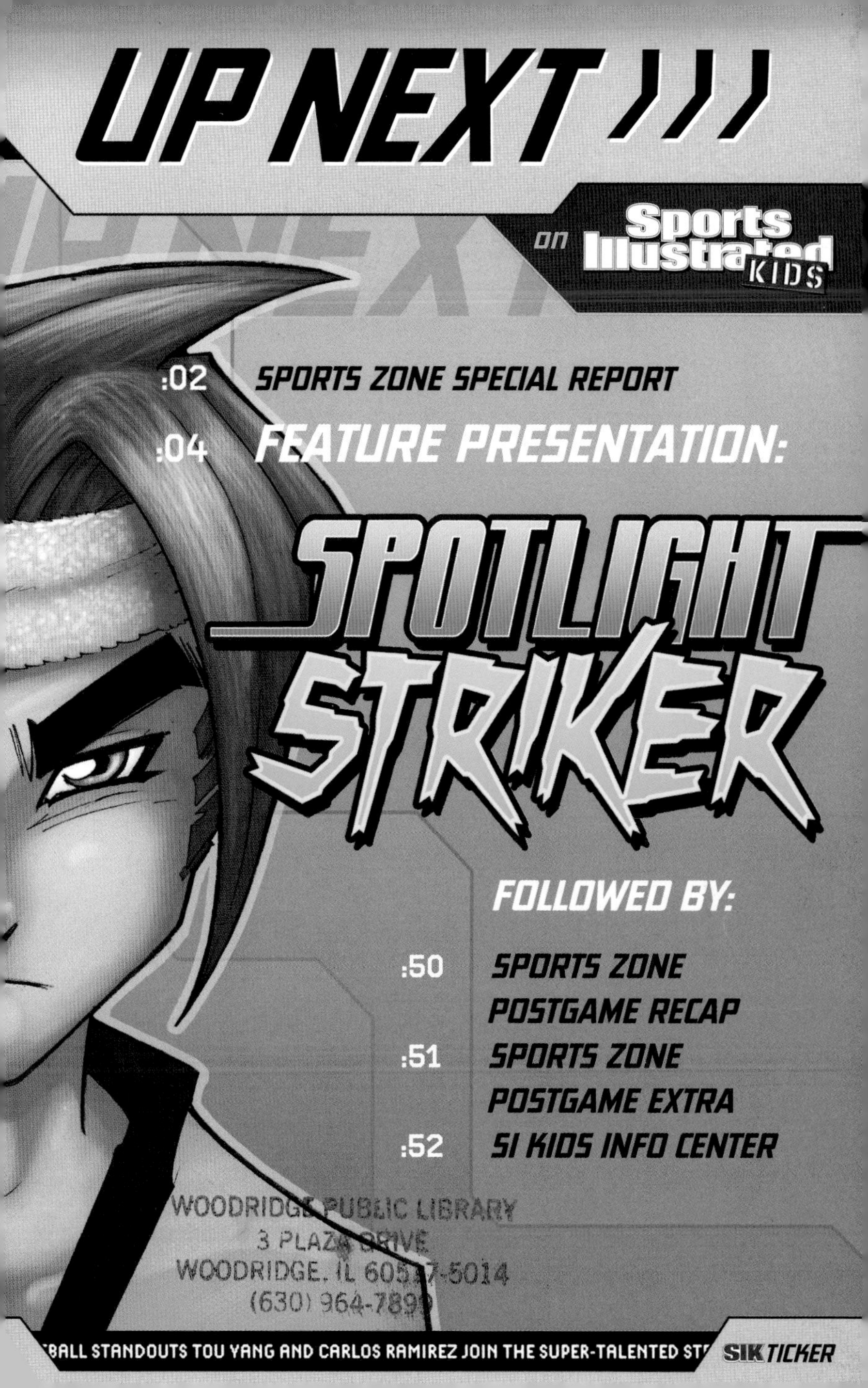
UP NEXT ›››
on Sports Illustrated KIDS
:02 SPORTS ZONE SPECIAL REPORT
:04 FEATURE PRESENTATION:
SPOTLIGHT STRIKER
FOLLOWED BY:
:50 SPORTS ZONE POSTGAME RECAP
:51 SPORTS ZONE POSTGAME EXTRA
:52 SI KIDS INFO CENTER
BALL STANDOUTS TOU YANG AND CARLOS RAMIREZ JOIN THE SUPER-TALENTED ST
SIK TICKER

SPORTS ZONE

ECIAL REPORT

STRIKERS' SUPERSTAR HIDES FROM SPOTLIGHT

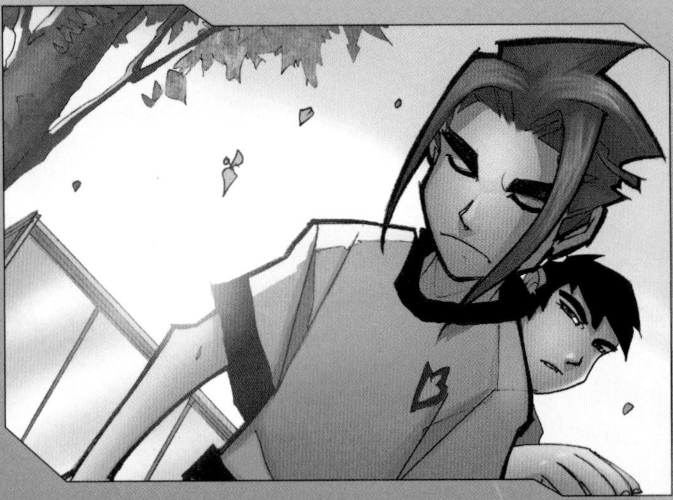

CARLOS RAMIREZ

STATS:
AGE: 14
TEAM: STRIKERS
POSITION: STRIKER

BIO: Carlos Ramirez impresses everyone with his lightning-fast reflexes, flashy kicks, and sneaky passes. He's a shoo-in for starting forward on varsity next year, and his grades are picture perfect. There's just one thing holding him back: when the pressure's on, Carlos prefers to be off the field. If this young star hopes to shine, he'll have to learn how to thrive in the spotlight.

UP NEXT: SPOTLIGHT STRIKER

TOU YANG

AGE: 14 TEAM: STRIKERS
POSITION: MIDFIELD

BIO: Tou is a small midfielder, but he has the confidence of a giant. When everyone else is ready to give up, Tou keeps their chins up, and their eyes on the ball. He is Carlos's best bud on and off the field.

BLZ vs BRS
3-1
TGR vs RDR
33-32
EAG vs BAN
14-7
SPA vs WLD
4-3
BAN vs RDR
21-15
RDR vs LIG
4-3
BLZ vs BRS
3-1
TGR vs RDR

RAMÓN RAMIREZ

AGE: 34

BIO: Ramón is a professional soccer player from Mexico. He hopes that his nephew, Carlos, will one day follow in his footsteps.

RAMIREZ

COACH DANIELS

AGE: 38 TEAM: STRIKERS

BIO: Coach Daniels expects team unity and hard work from all his Strikers. To him, giving it everything you've got is all that matters.

COACH

MARTA RAMIREZ

AGE: 44

BIO: Mrs. Ramirez is Carlos's mother. Her younger brother, Ramón, is a big part of their lives.

MRS. RAMIREZ

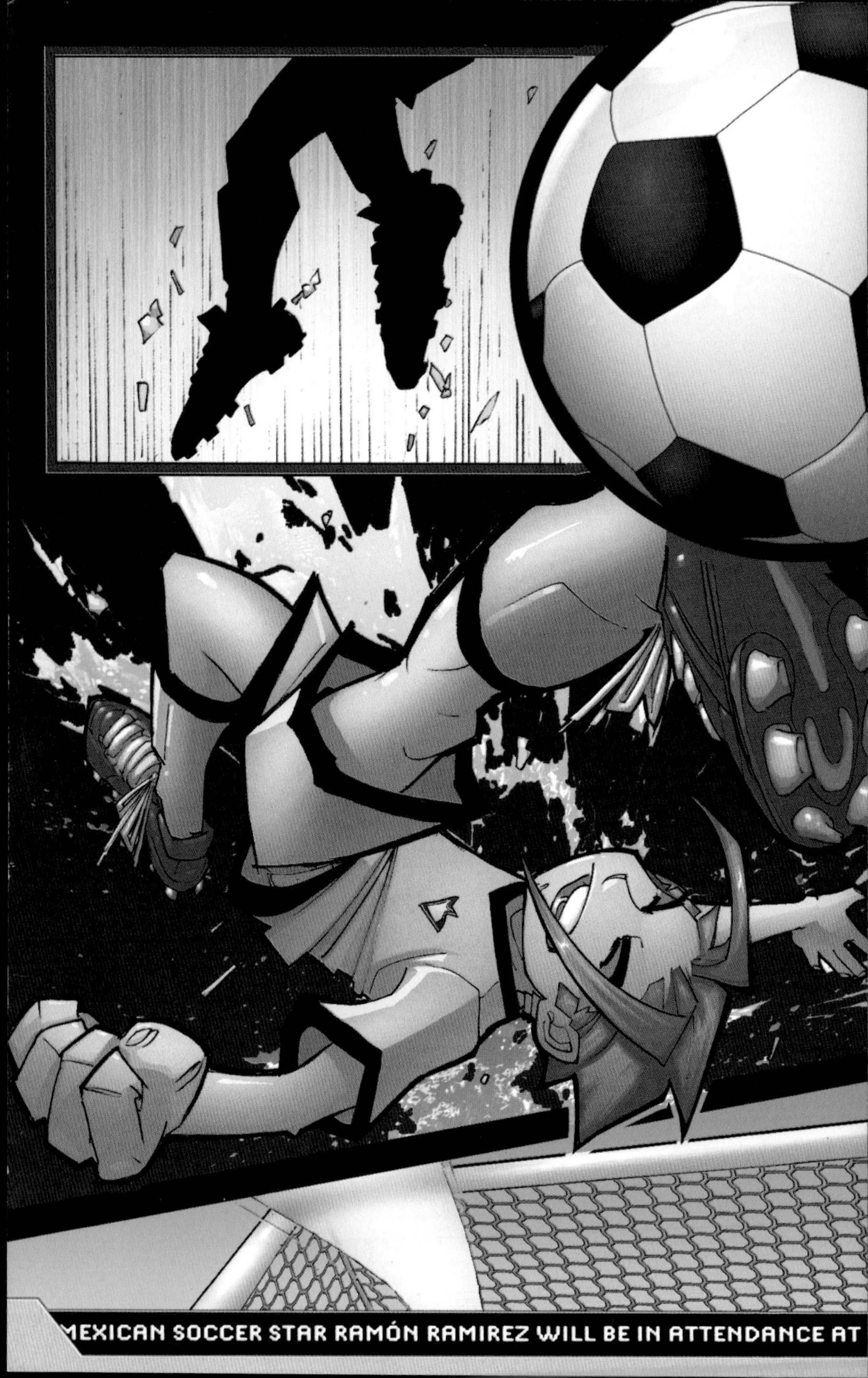
MEXICAN SOCCER STAR RAMÓN RAMIREZ WILL BE IN ATTENDANCE AT

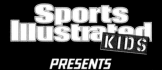

Sports Illustrated KIDS

PRESENTS

SPOTLIGHT STRIKER

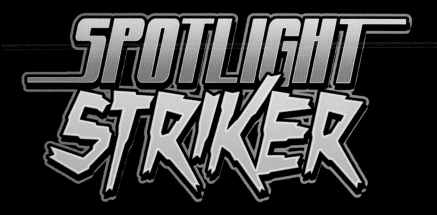

A PRODUCTION OF

STONE ARCH BOOKS
a capstone imprint

written by Blake A. Hoena
illustrated by Gerardo Sandoval
colored by Benny Fuentes

designed and directed by Bob Lentz
edited by Sean Tulien
creative direction by Heather Kindseth
editorial direction by Michael Dahl

Sports Illustrated KIDS *Spotlight Striker* is published by Stone Arch Books,
151 Good Counsel Drive, P.O. Box 669, Mankato, Minnesota 56002.
www.capstonepub.com

Summary: Carlos Ramirez has always been the Strikers' best scorer. But the state's best team is coming to town, and Carlos hears that he'll have a very special fan in the stands. His uncle, a professional soccer player, will be watching his nephew's every move during the Strikers' biggest game of the year. As the pressure begins to set in, Carlos struggles to even hit the ball. Everyone has seen that Carlos is a gifted athlete, but no one knows whether he'll shine as the center of attention, or be blinded by the spotlight.

Cataloging-in-Publication Data is available at the Library of Congress website.

ISBN: 978-1-4342-2128-5 (library binding)
ISBN: 978-1-4342-2787-4 (paperback)

Printed in the United States of America in Stevens Point, Wisconsin.
122012 007083R

END'S SOCCER SHOWDOWN BETWEEN STRIKERS AND BANDIT SIK TICKER

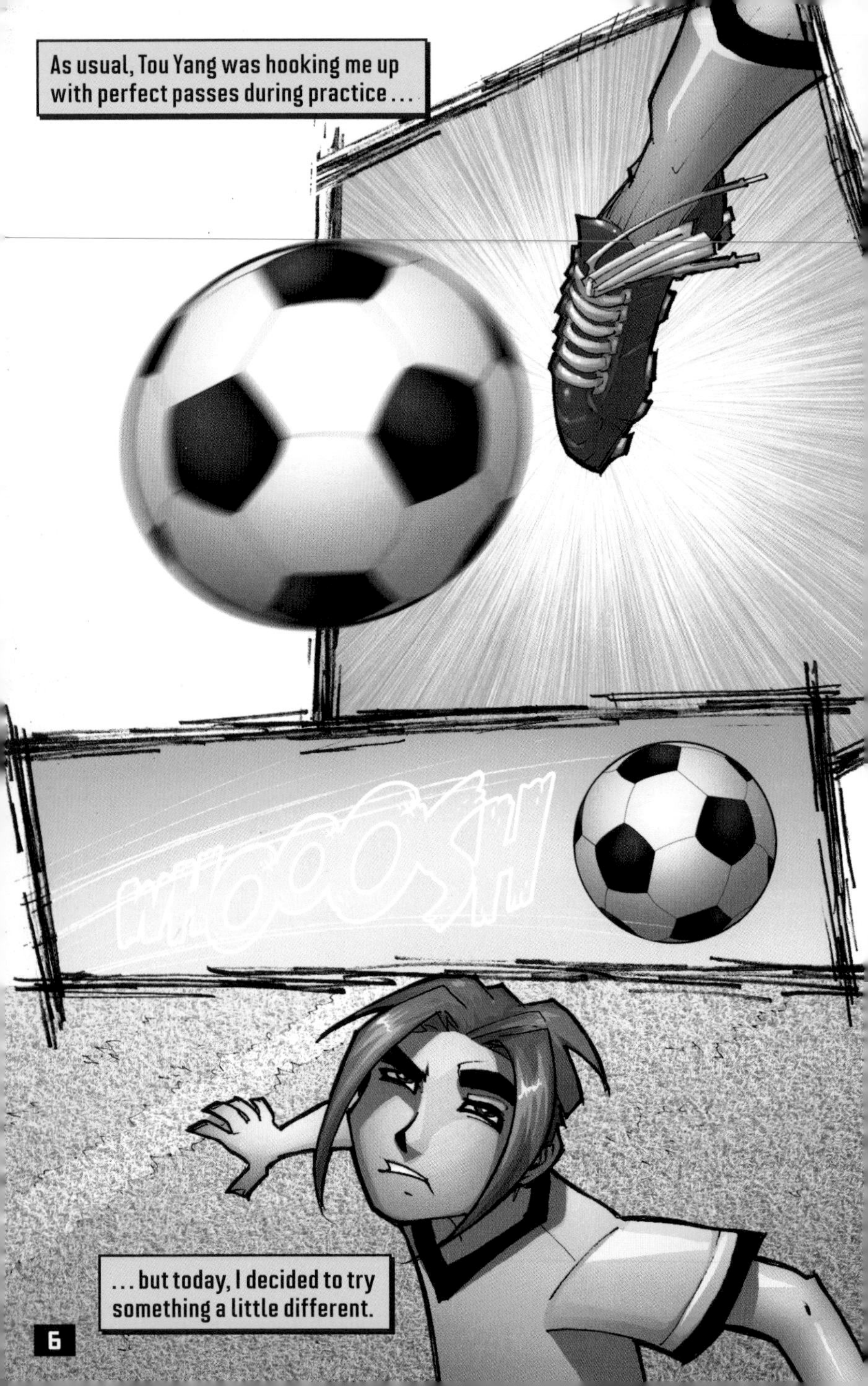
As usual, Tou Yang was hooking me up with perfect passes during practice . . .
WHOOOSH
. . . but today, I decided to try something a little different.

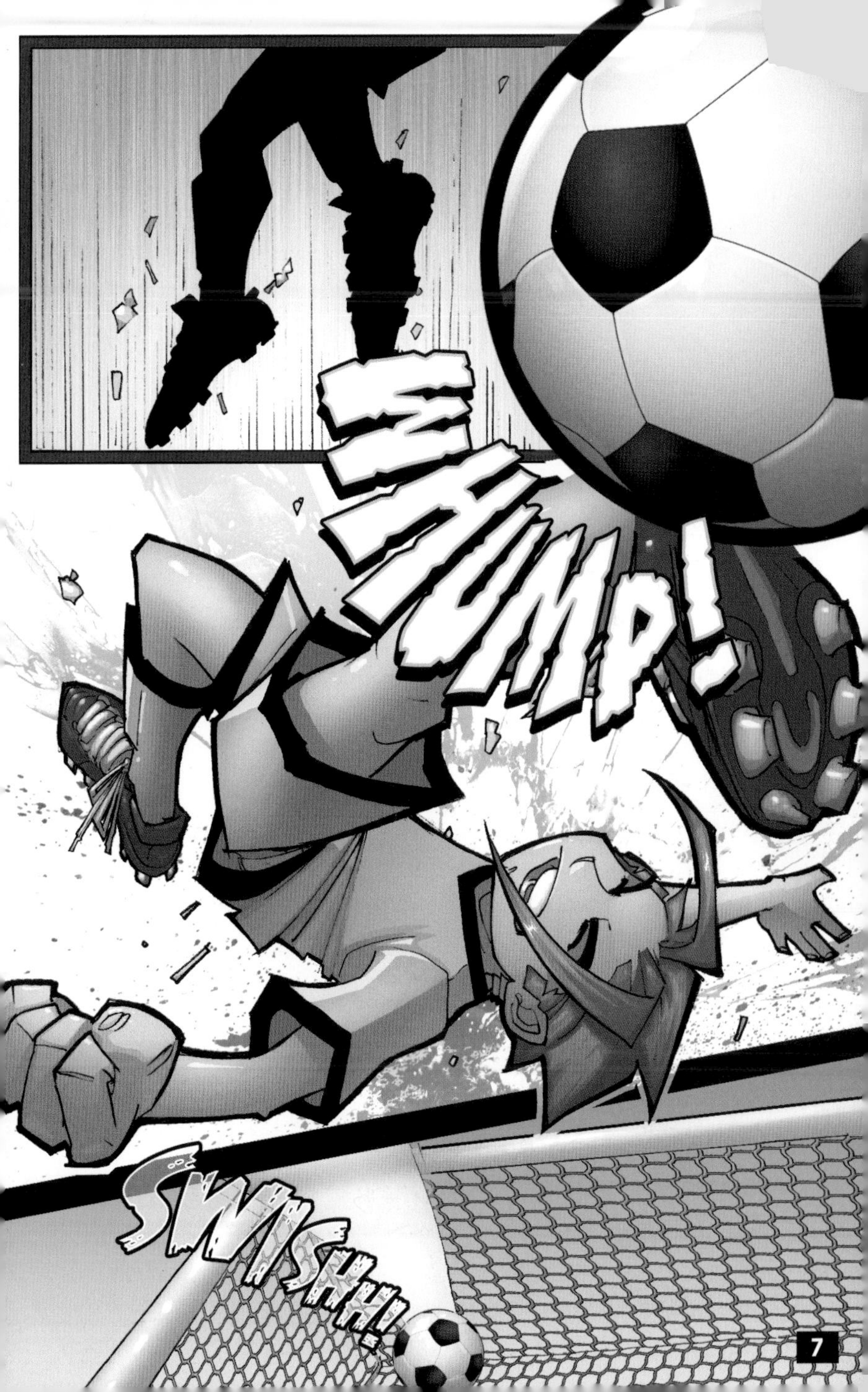
THUMP!
SWISHH!

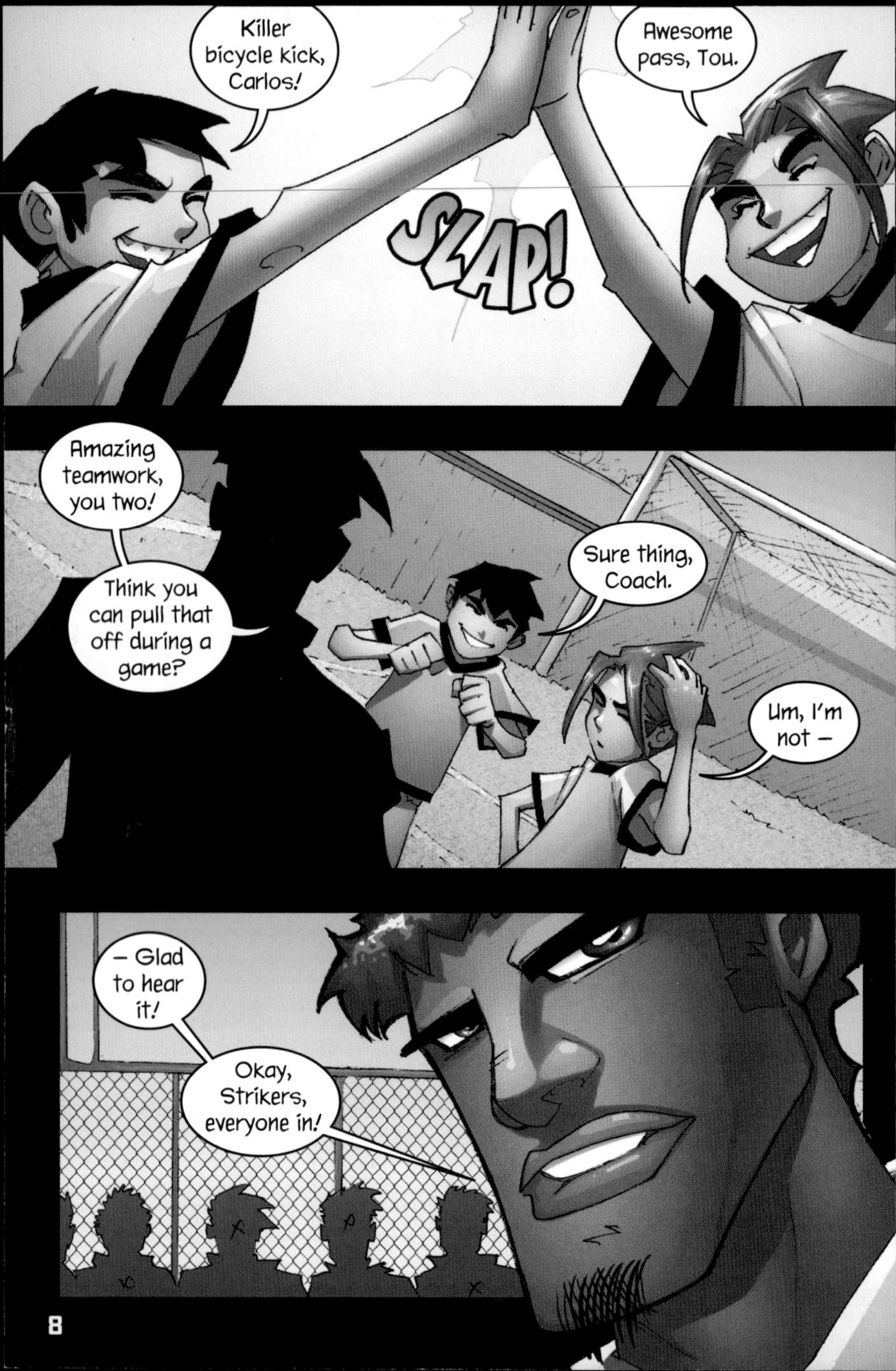
Killer bicycle kick, Carlos!
Awesome pass, Tou.
SLAP!
Amazing teamwork, you two!
Think you can pull that off during a game?
Sure thing, Coach.
Um, I'm not –
– Glad to hear it!
Okay, Strikers, everyone in!

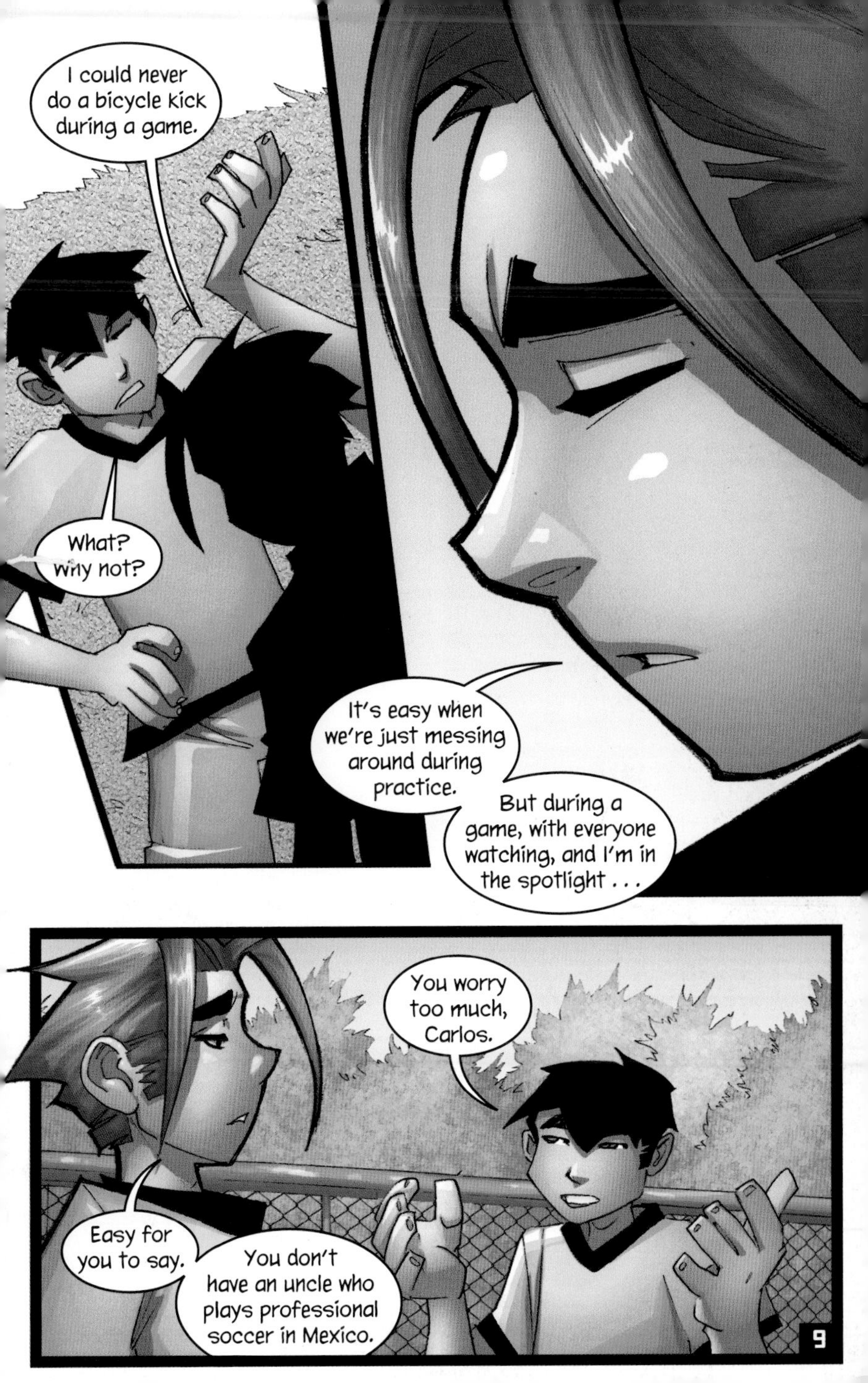
I could never do a bicycle kick during a game.
What? Why not?
It's easy when we're just messing around during practice.
But during a game, with everyone watching, and I'm in the spotlight . . .
You worry too much, Carlos.
Easy for you to say.
You don't have an uncle who plays professional soccer in Mexico.
9

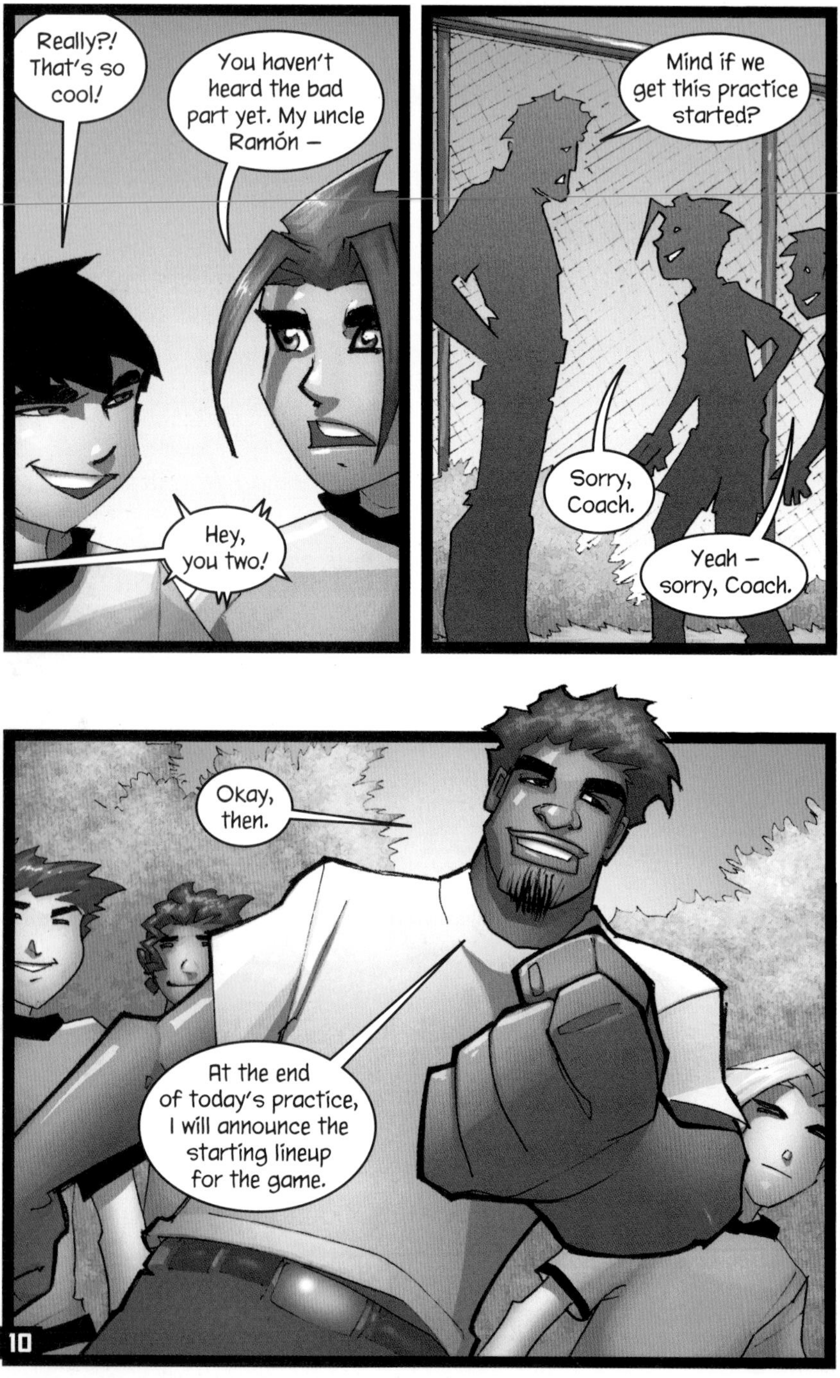
Really?! That's so cool!
You haven't heard the bad part yet. My uncle Ramón –
Hey, you two!
Mind if we get this practice started?
Sorry, Coach.
Yeah – sorry, Coach.
Okay, then.
At the end of today's practice, I will announce the starting lineup for the game.

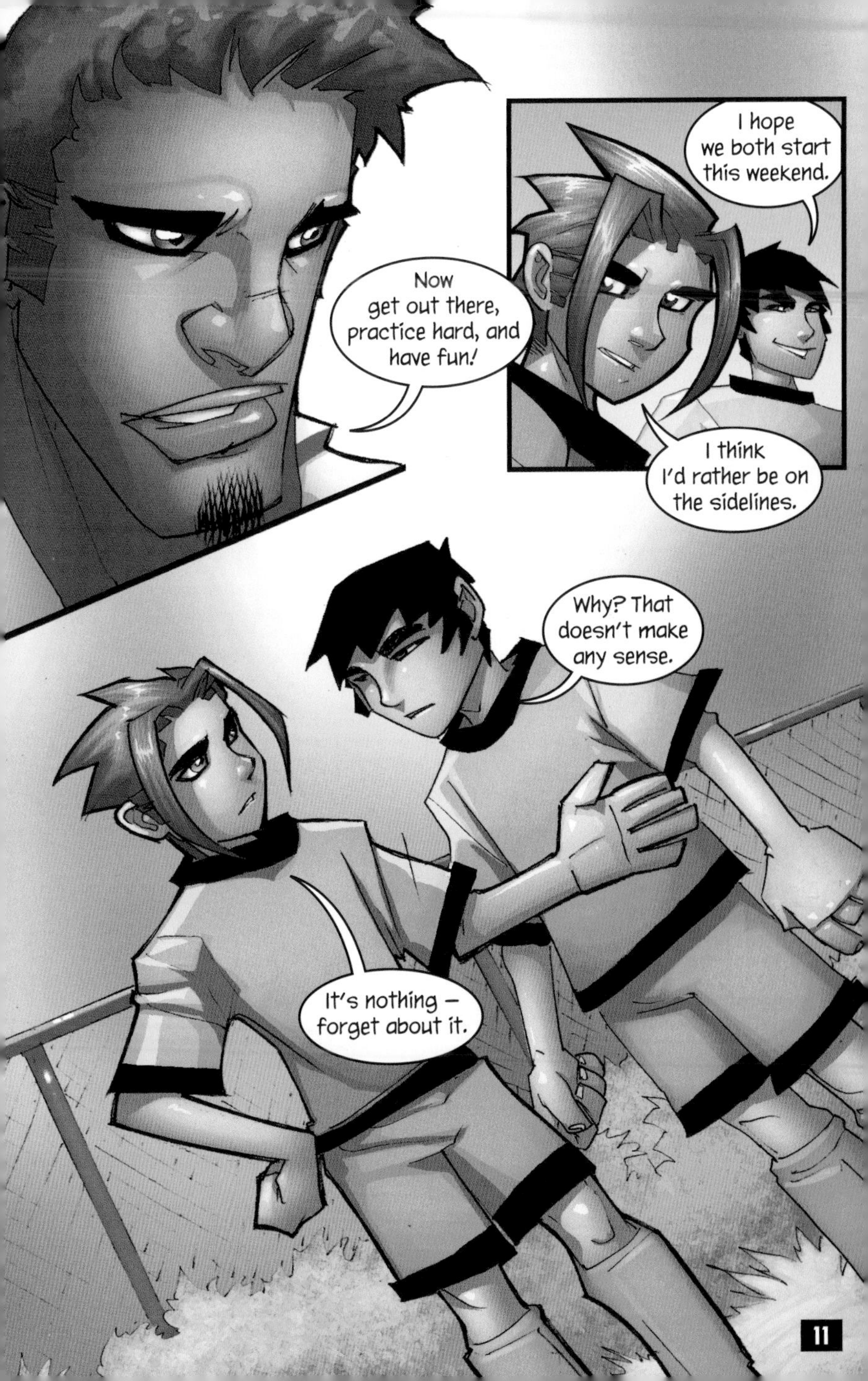
Now get out there, practice hard, and have fun!
I hope we both start this weekend.
I think I'd rather be on the sidelines.
Why? That doesn't make any sense.
It's nothing — forget about it.

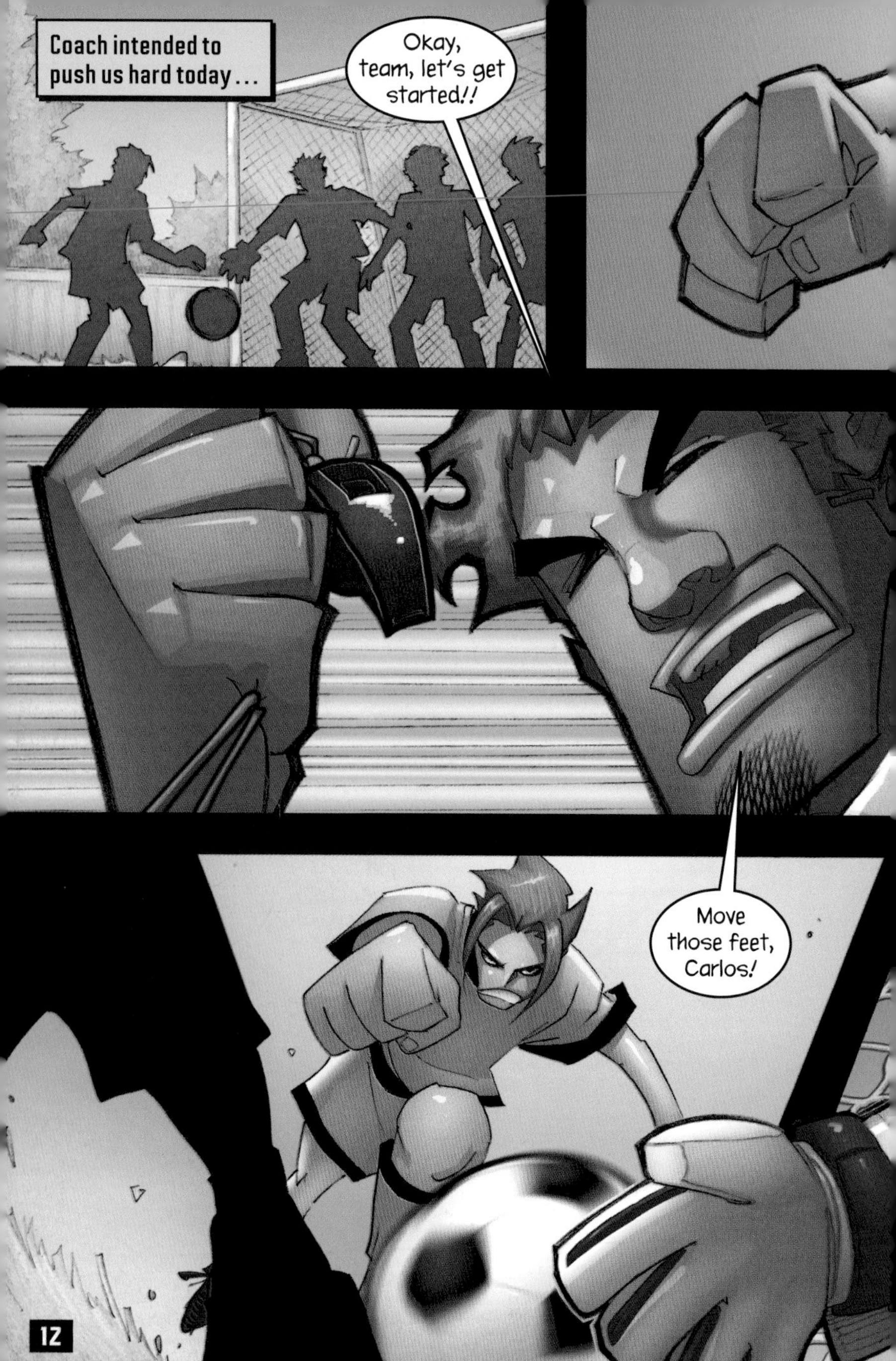

Coach intended to push us hard today . . .
Okay, team, let's get started!!
Move those feet, Carlos!

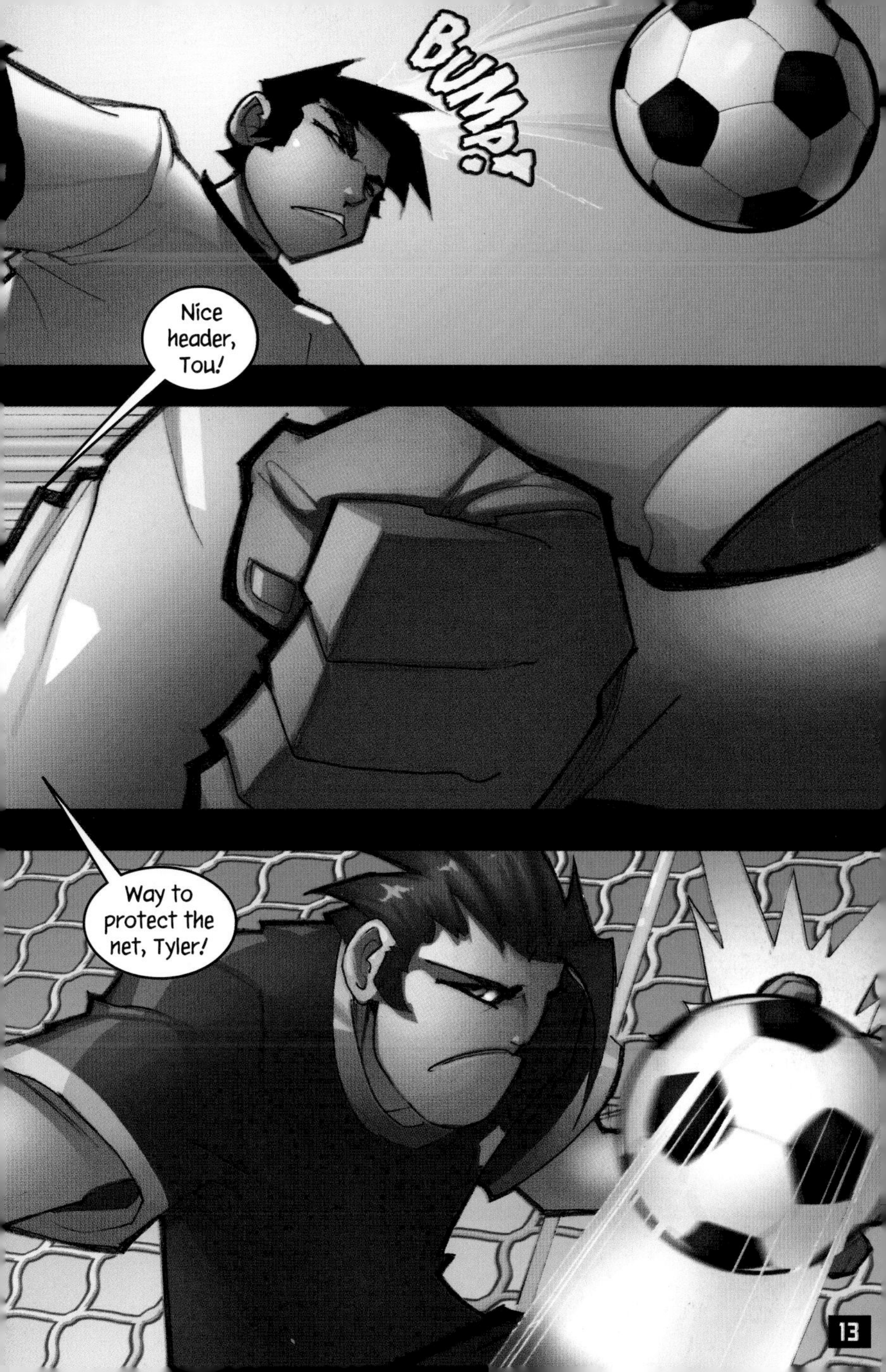
BUMP!
Nice header, Tou!
Way to protect the net, Tyler!

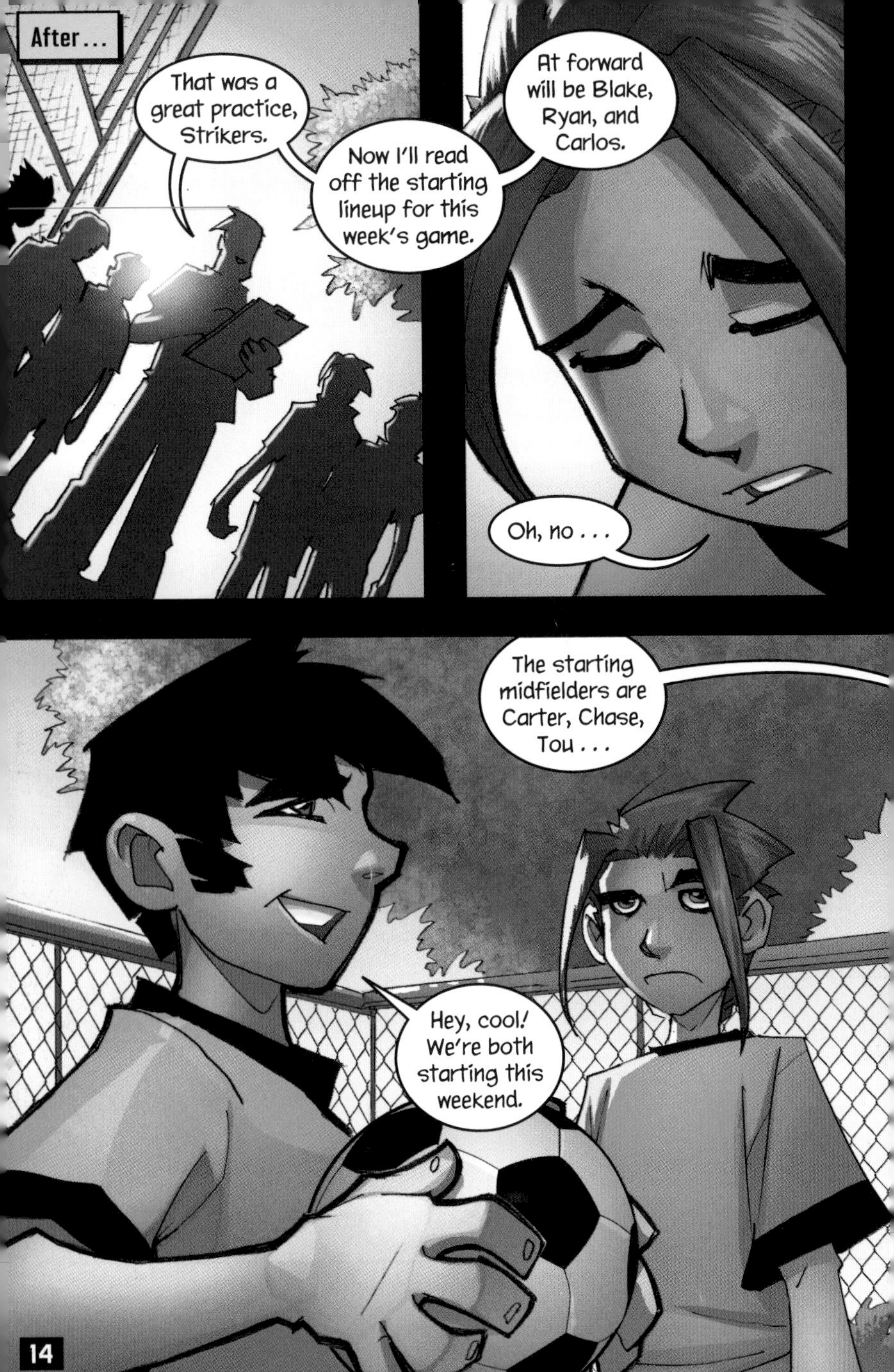
After . . .
That was a great practice, Strikers.
Now I'll read off the starting lineup for this week's game.
At forward will be Blake, Ryan, and Carlos.
Oh, no . . .
The starting midfielders are Carter, Chase, Tou . . .
Hey, cool! We're both starting this weekend.

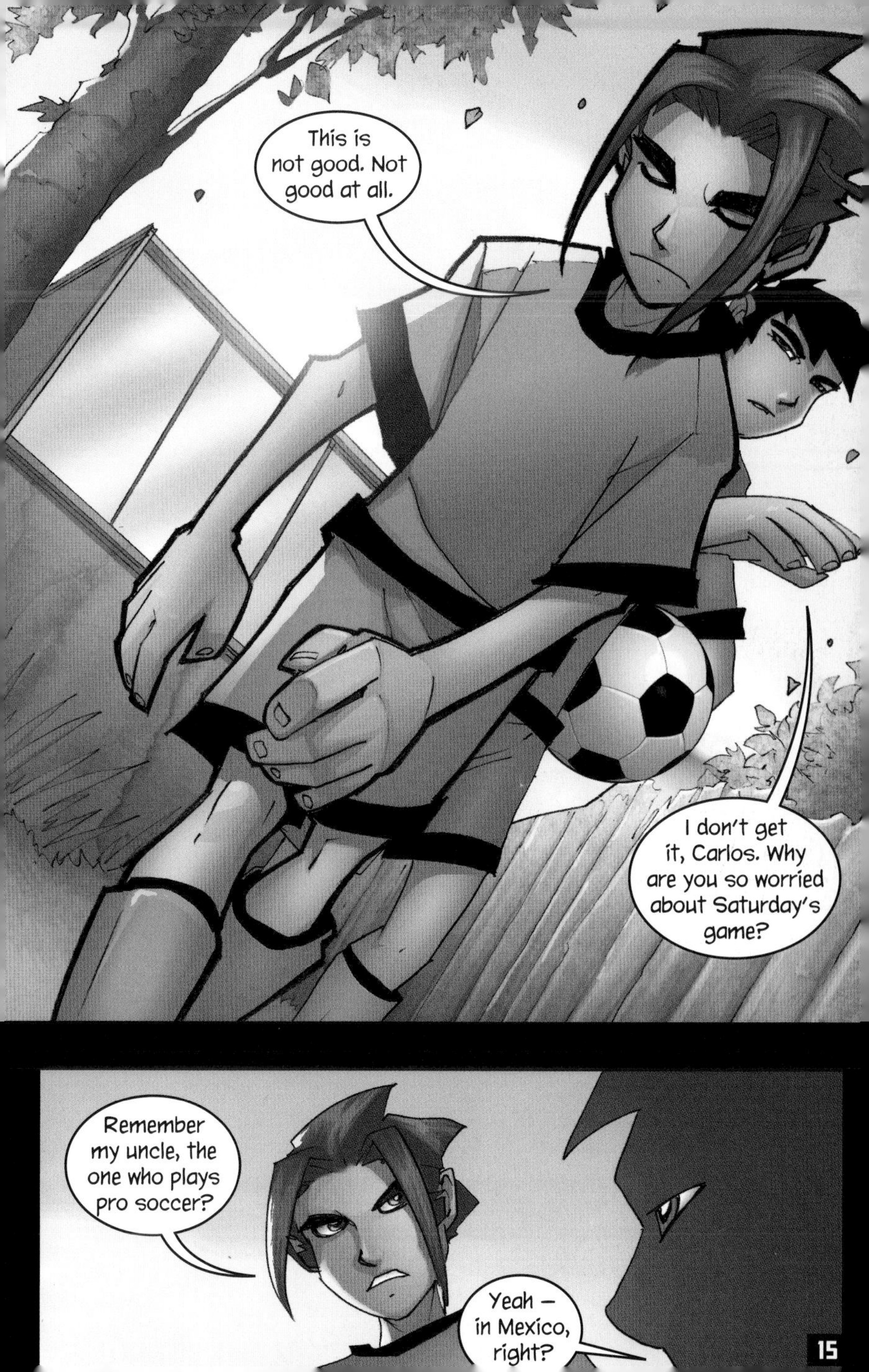
This is not good. Not good at all.
I don't get it, Carlos. Why are you so worried about Saturday's game?
Remember my uncle, the one who plays pro soccer?
Yeah — in Mexico, right?

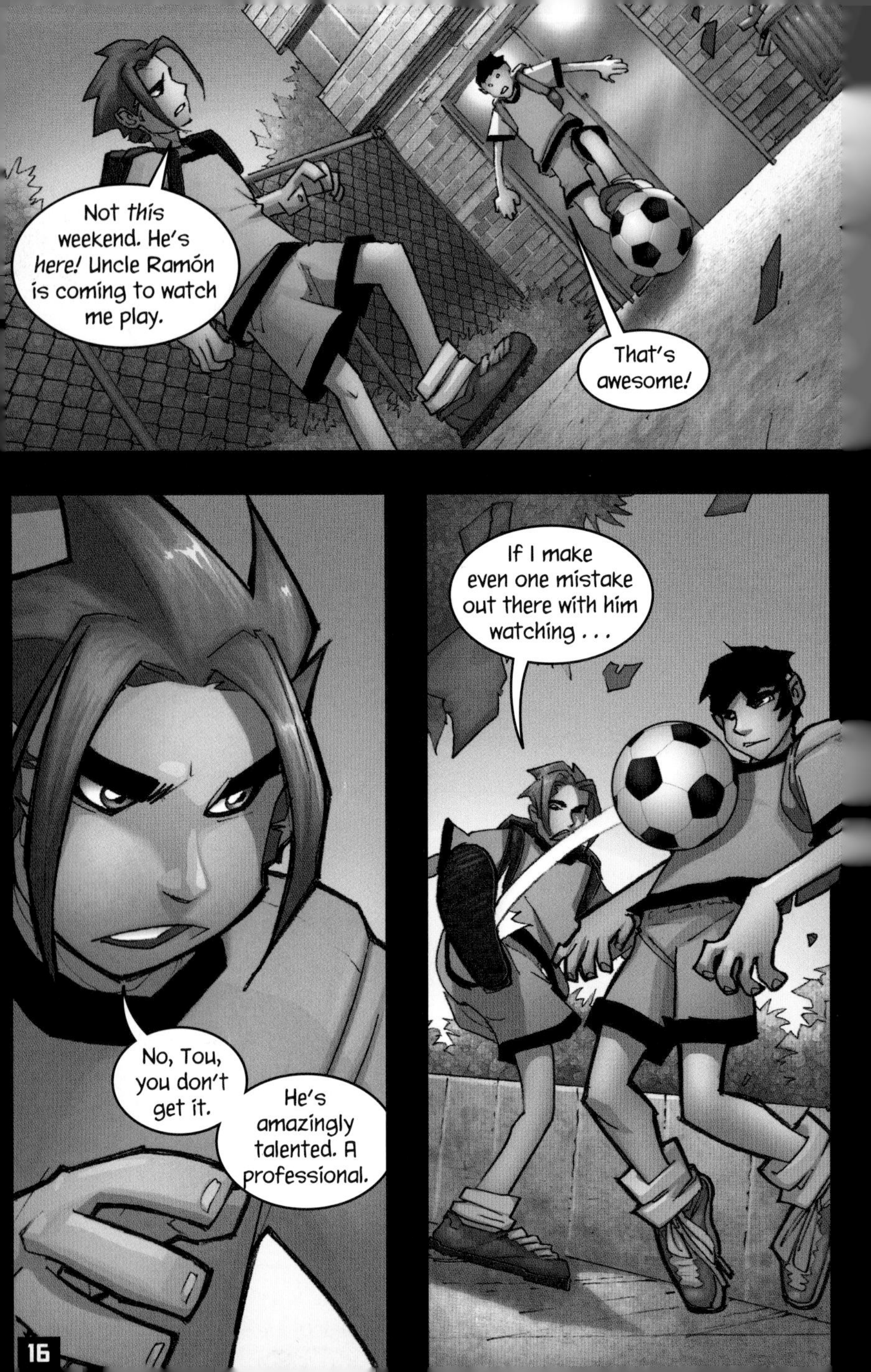

Not this weekend. He's *here!* Uncle Ramón is coming to watch me play.
That's awesome!
No, Tou, you don't get it.
He's amazingly talented. A professional.
If I make even one mistake out there with him watching . . .

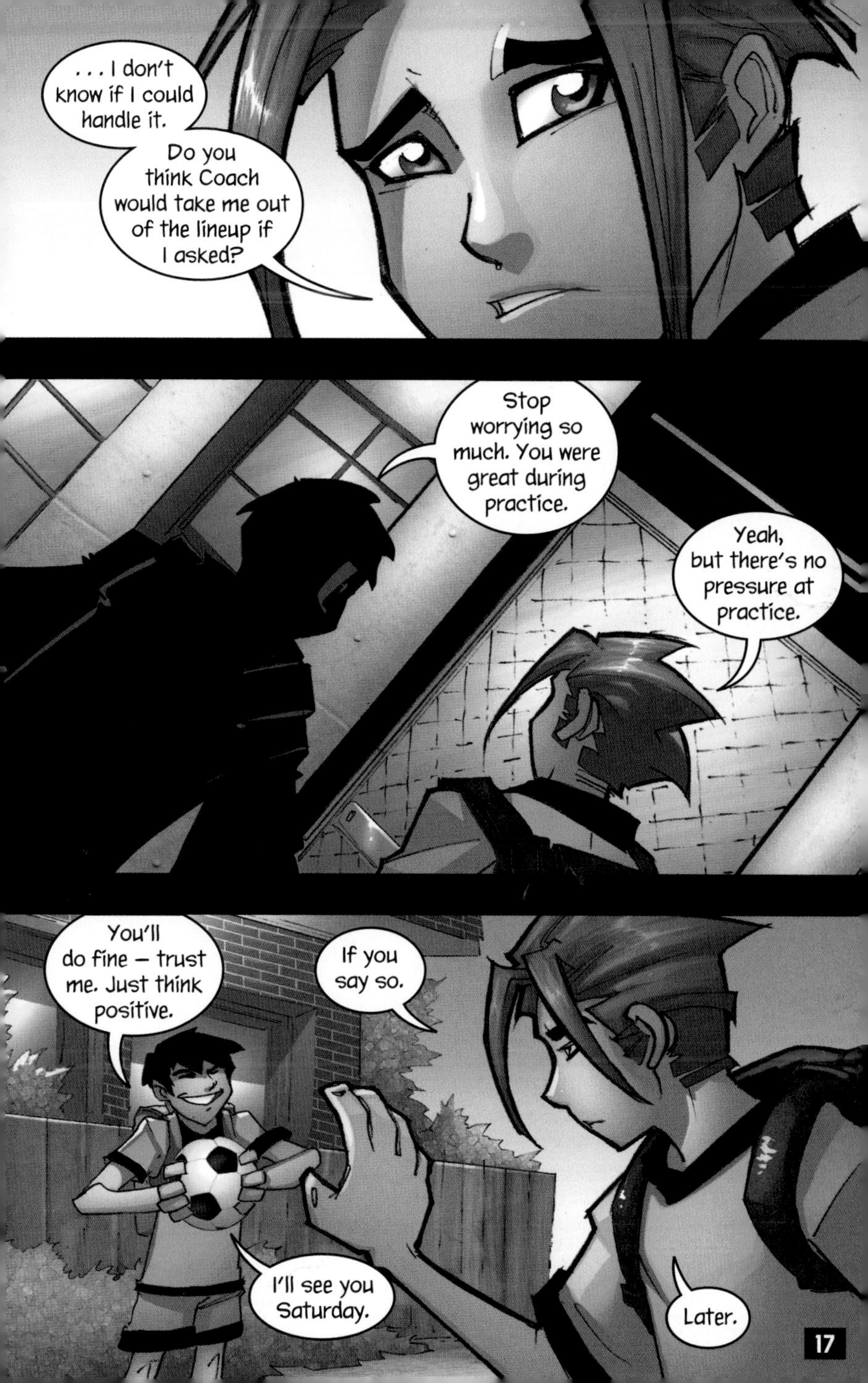

. . . I don't know if I could handle it.
Do you think Coach would take me out of the lineup if I asked?
Stop worrying so much. You were great during practice.
Yeah, but there's no pressure at practice.
You'll do fine — trust me. Just think positive.
If you say so.
I'll see you Saturday.
Later.

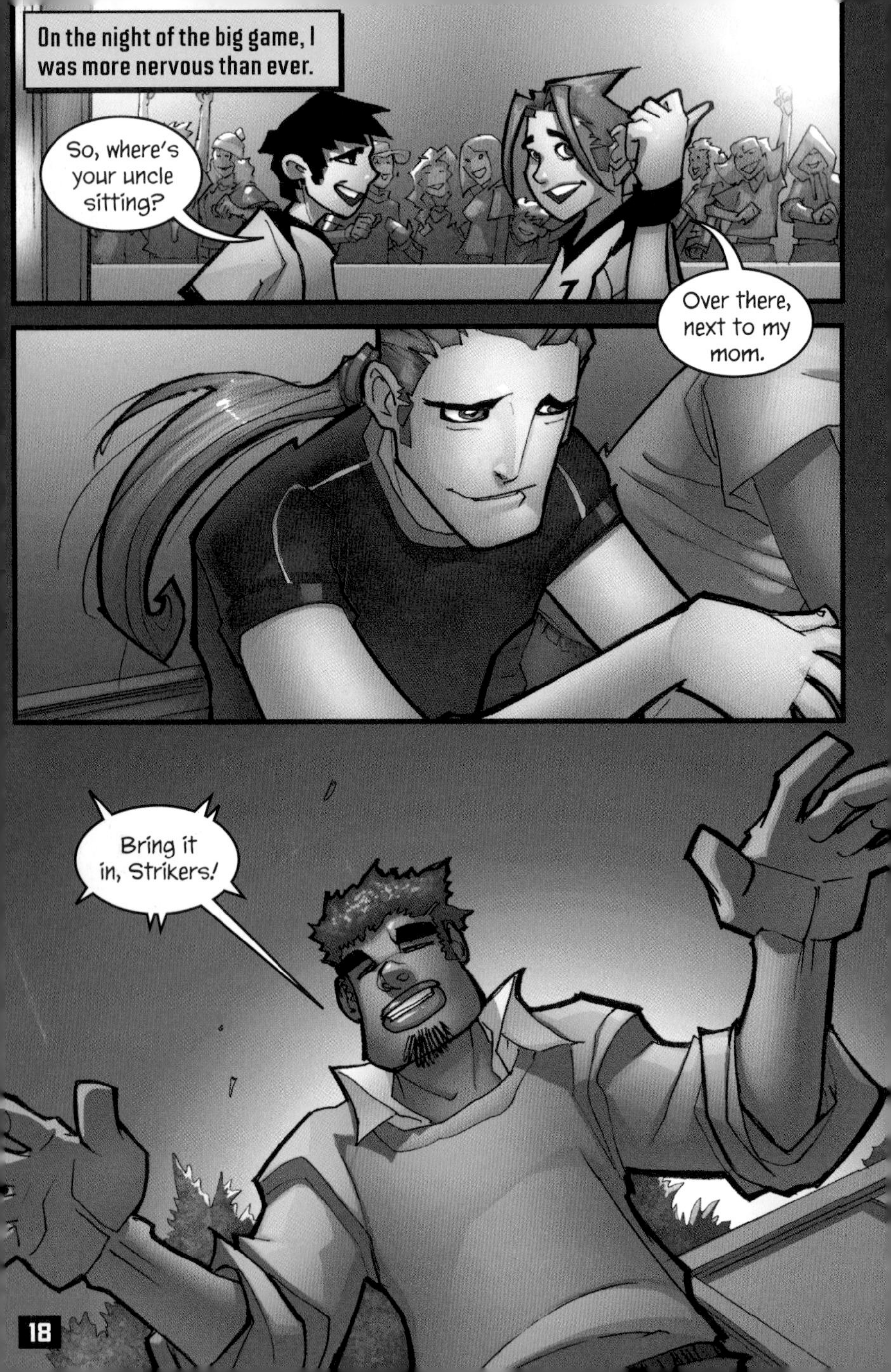
On the night of the big game, I was more nervous than ever.
So, where's your uncle sitting?
Over there, next to my mom.
Bring it in, Strikers!

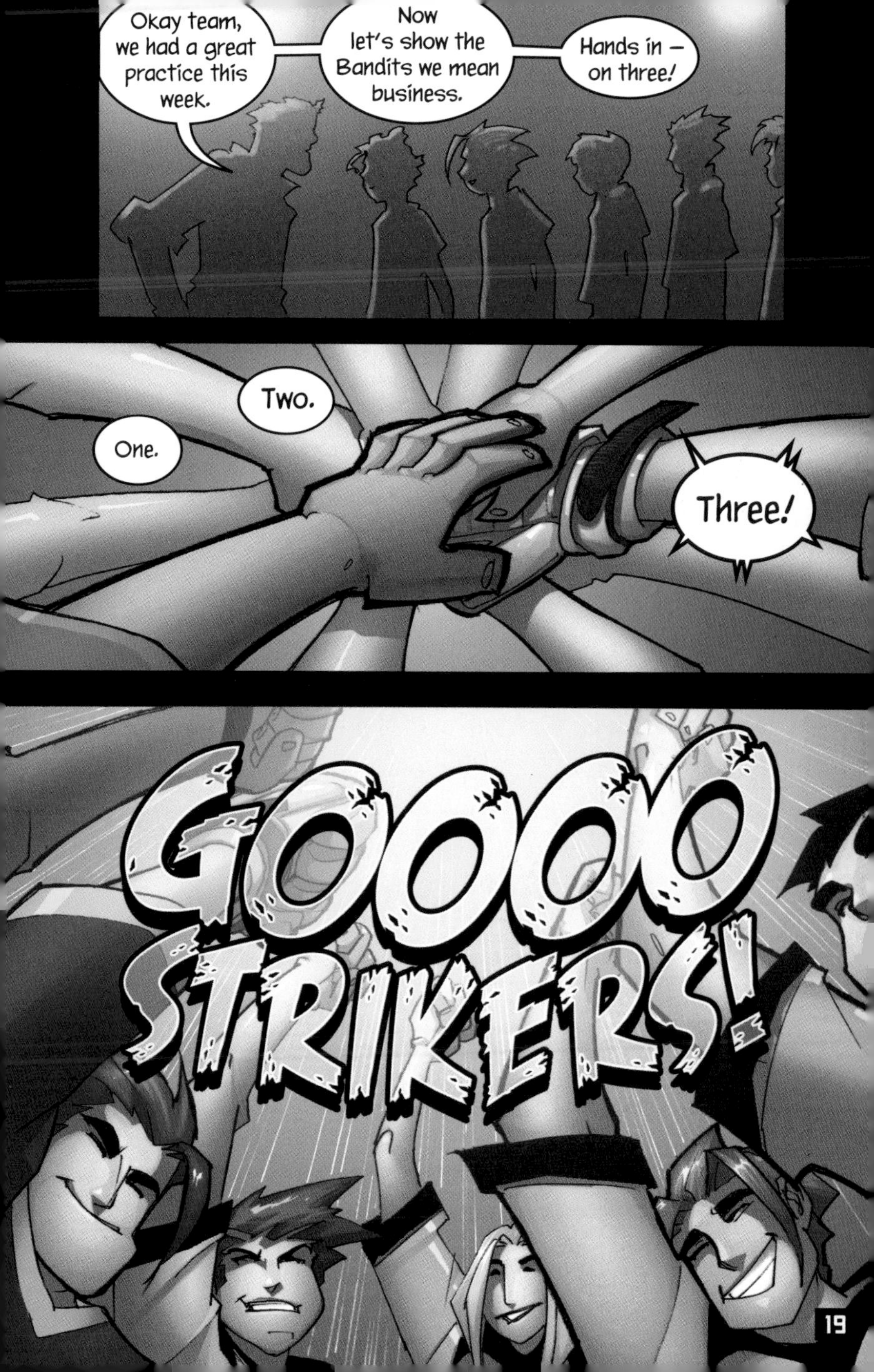
Okay team, we had a great practice this week.
Now let's show the Bandits we mean business.
Hands in — on three!
One.
Two.
Three!
GOOOO STRIKERS!

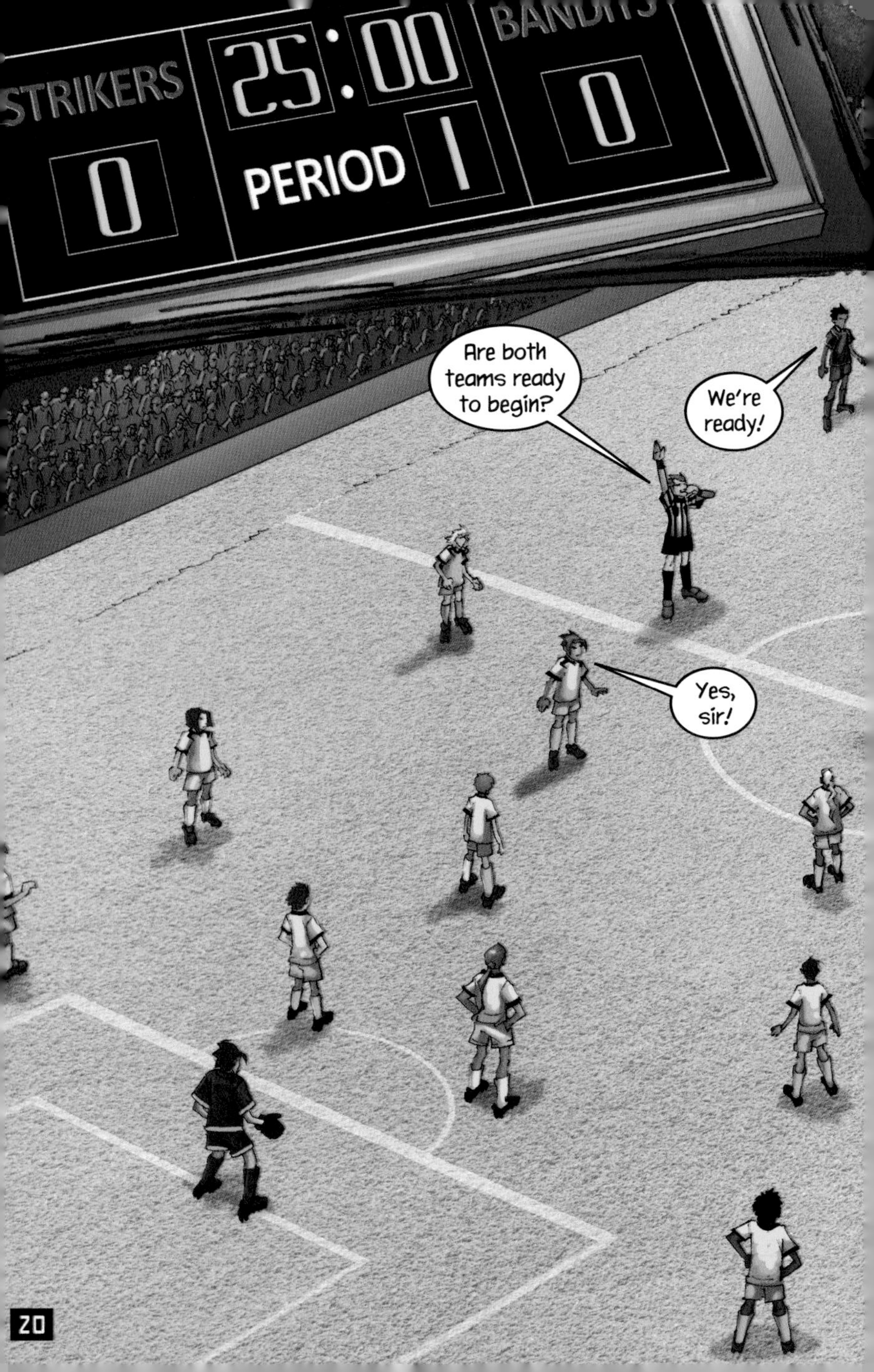
STRIKERS
25:00
BANDITS
0
PERIOD 1
0
Are both teams ready to begin?
We're ready!
Yes, sir!

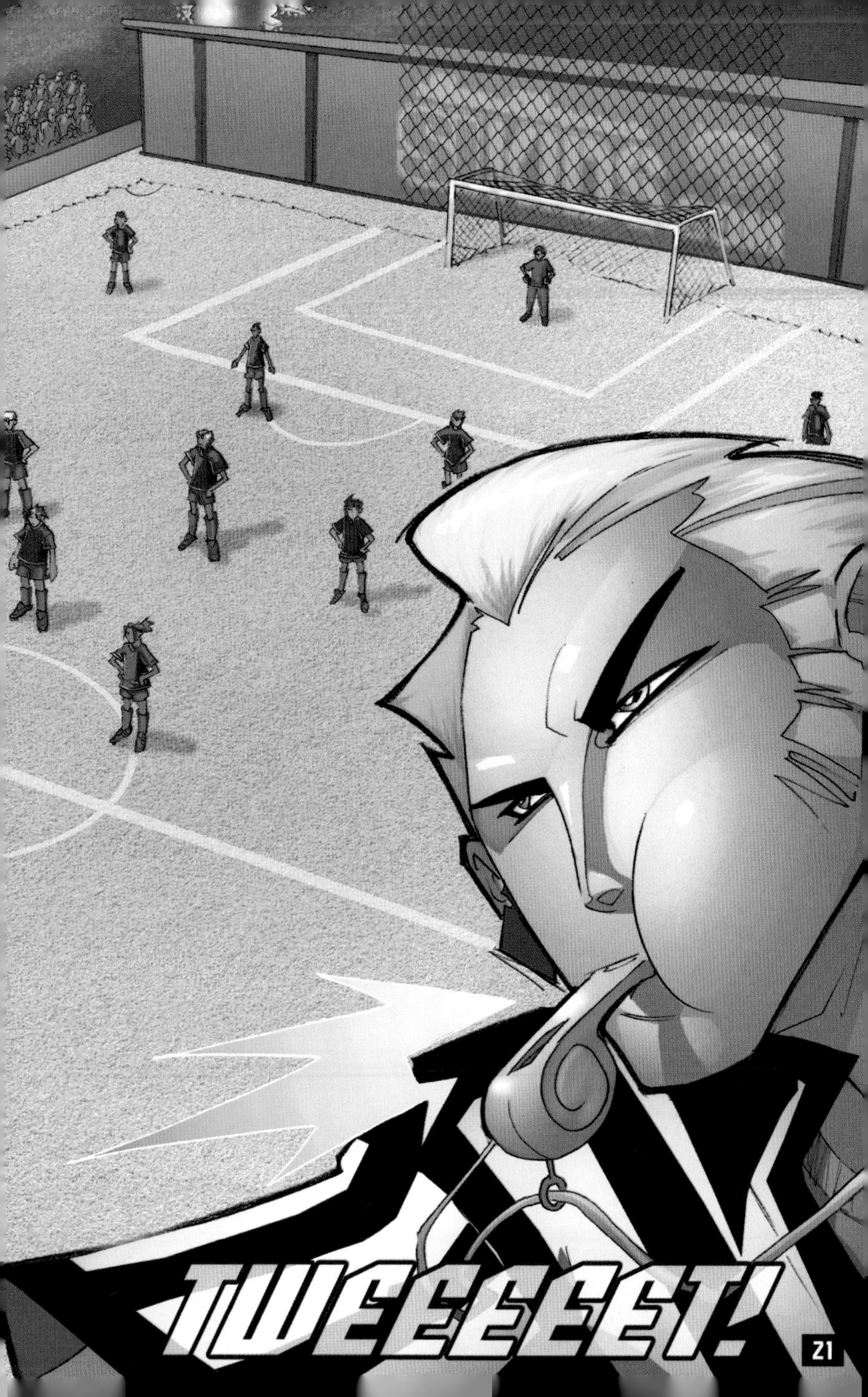
TWEEEEET!

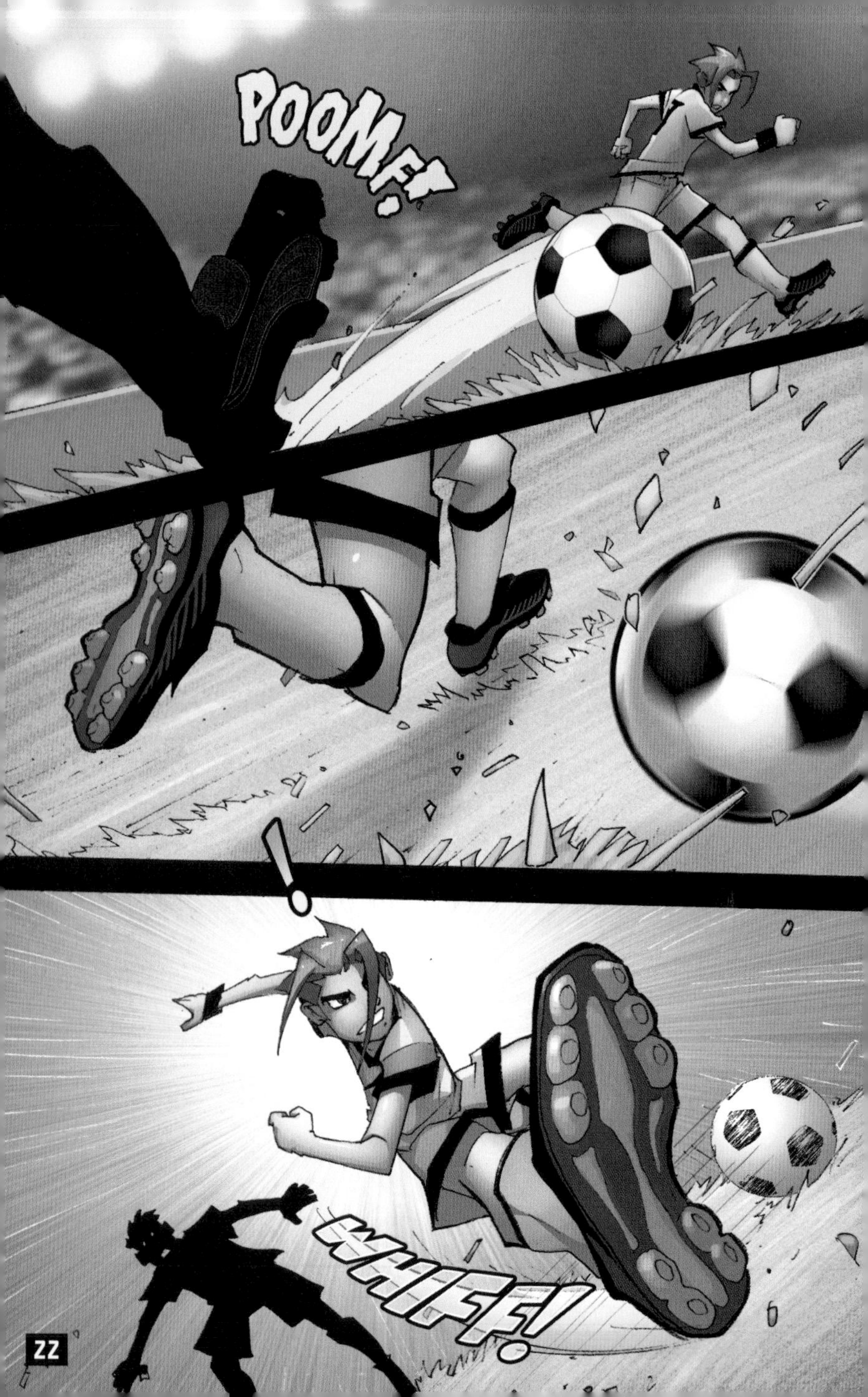
POOMF!
!
WHIFF!

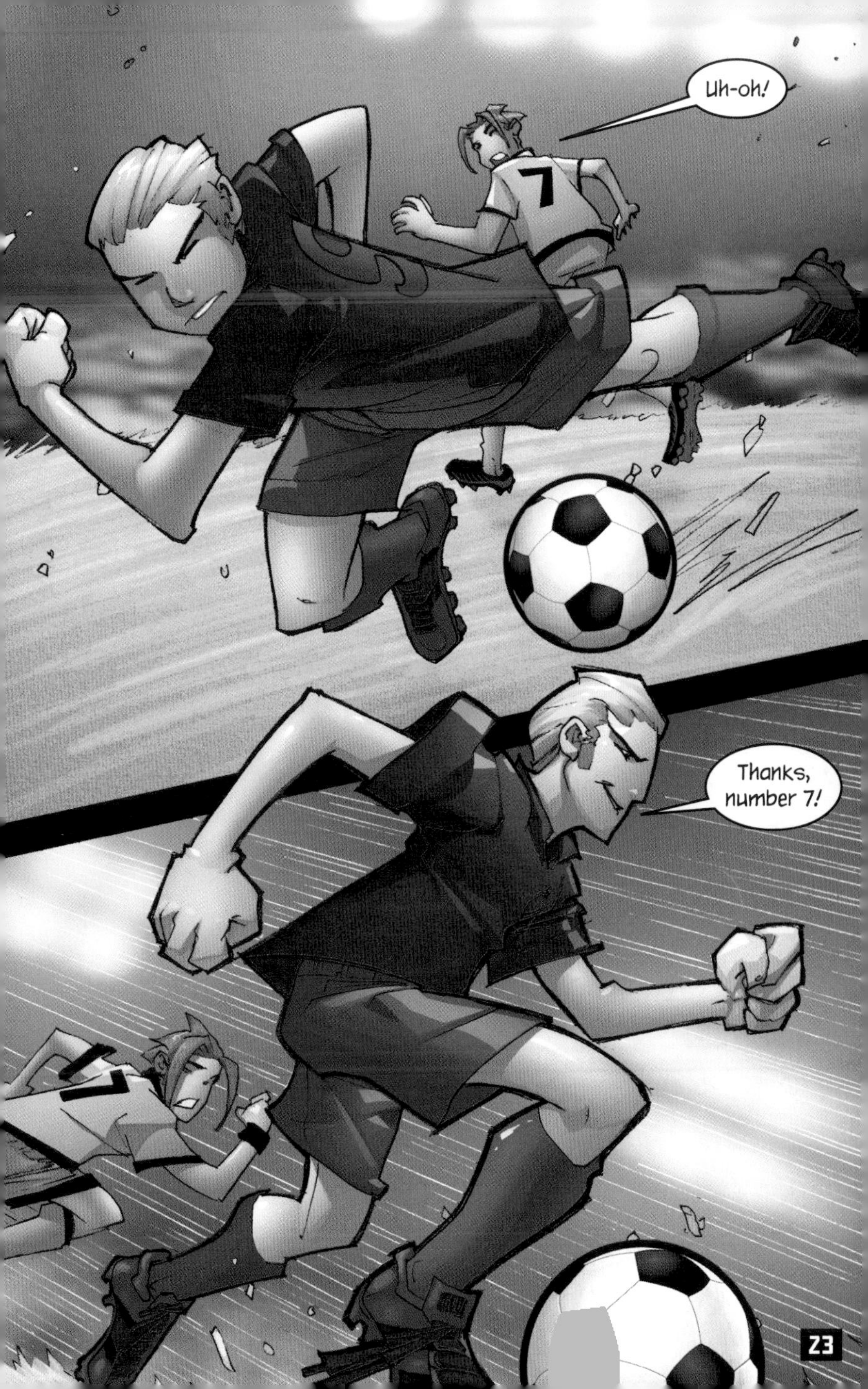
Uh-oh!
Thanks, number 7!

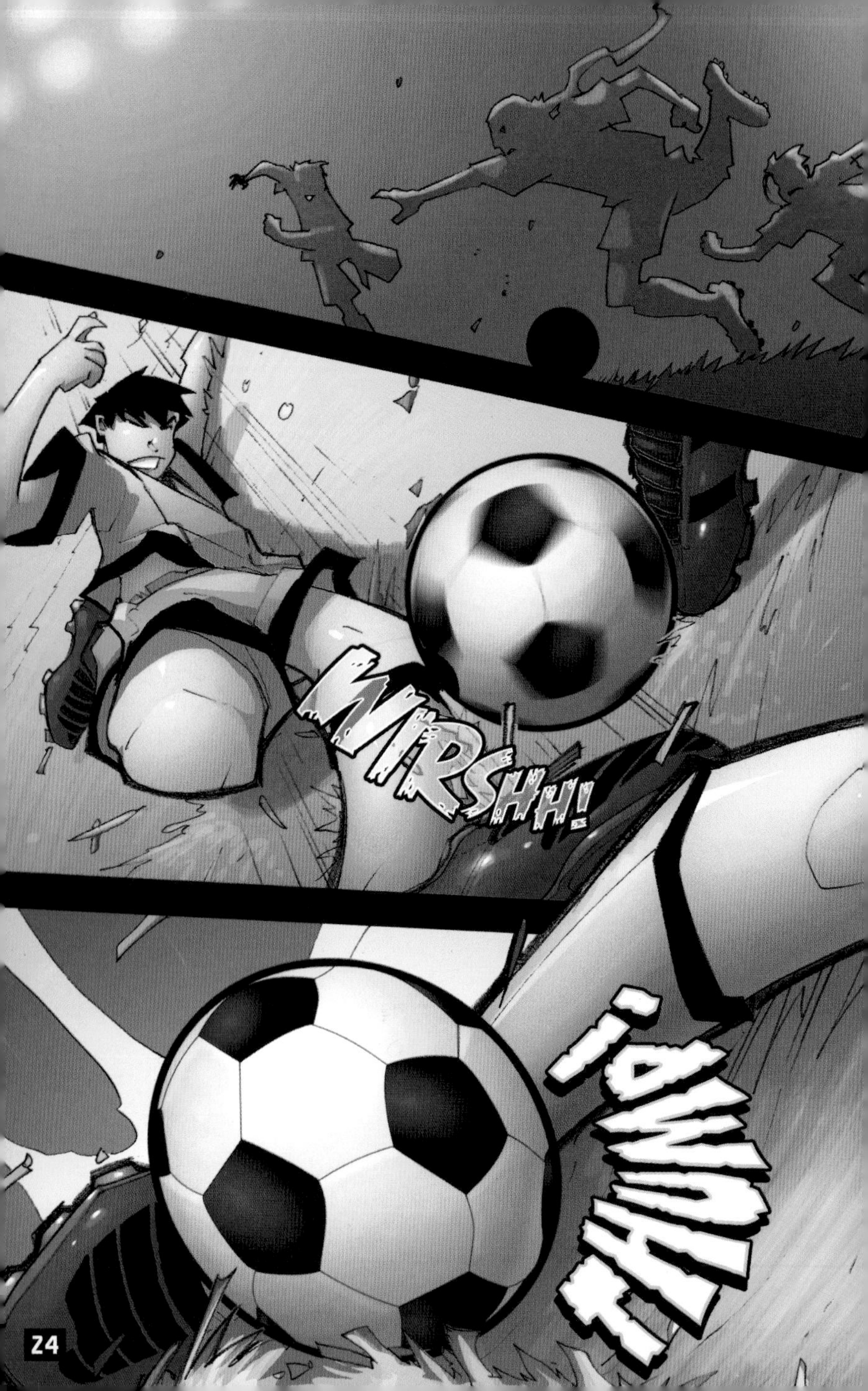
WIRSHH!
THWUMP!

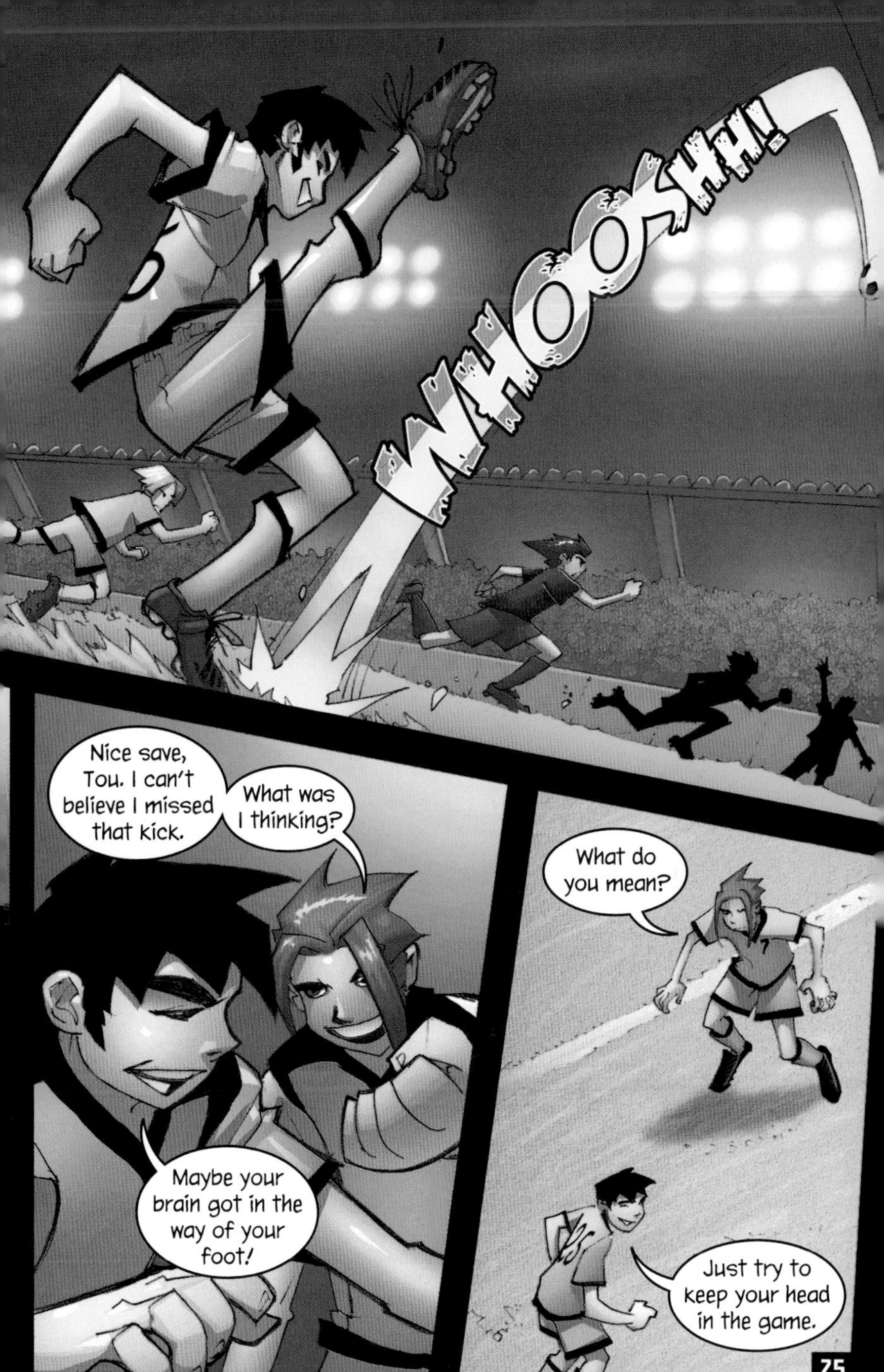
WHOOSHH!
Nice save, Tou. I can't believe I missed that kick.
What was I thinking?
Maybe your brain got in the way of your foot!
What do you mean?
Just try to keep your head in the game.

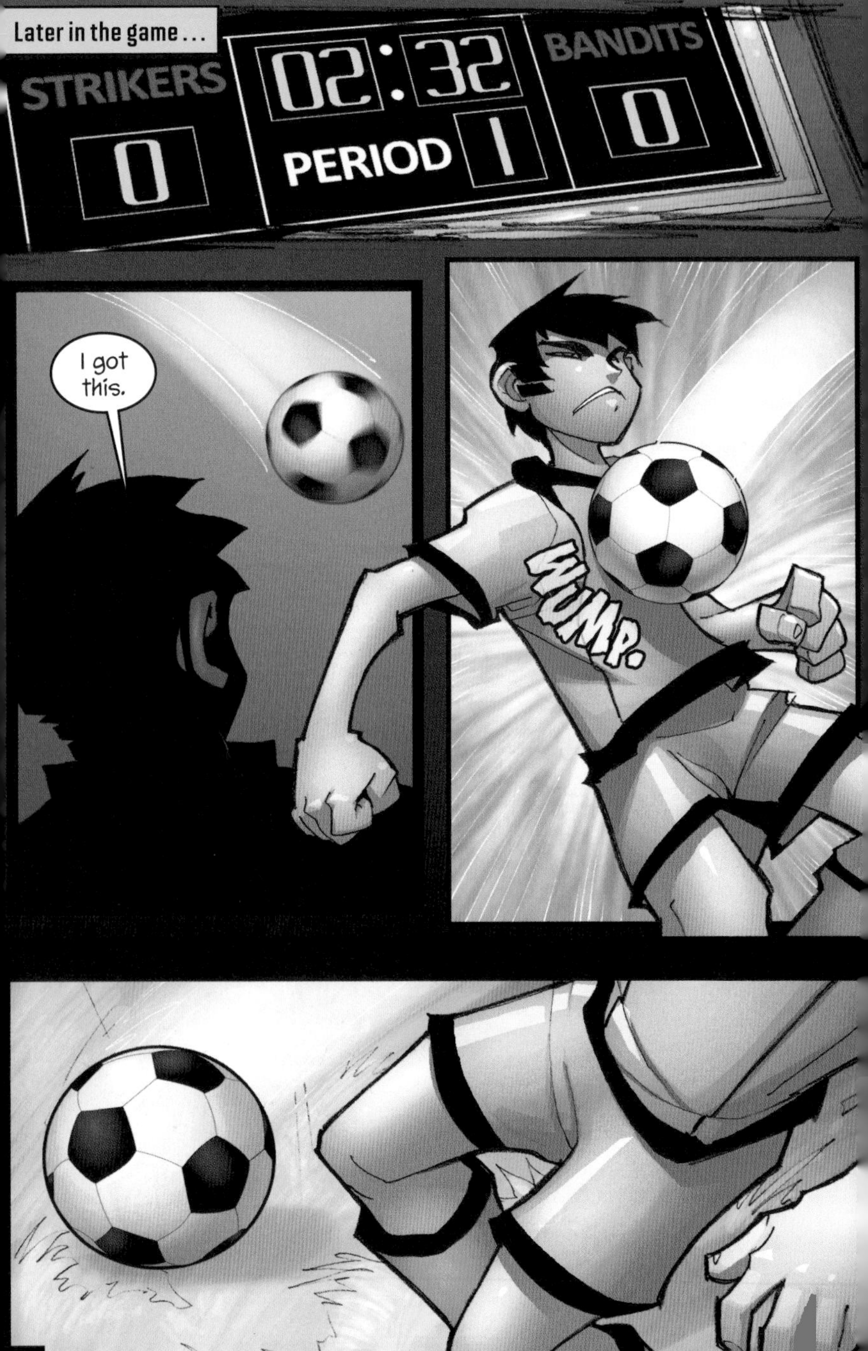
Later in the game . . .
STRIKERS
0
02:32
PERIOD 1
BANDITS
0
I got this.
WUMP.

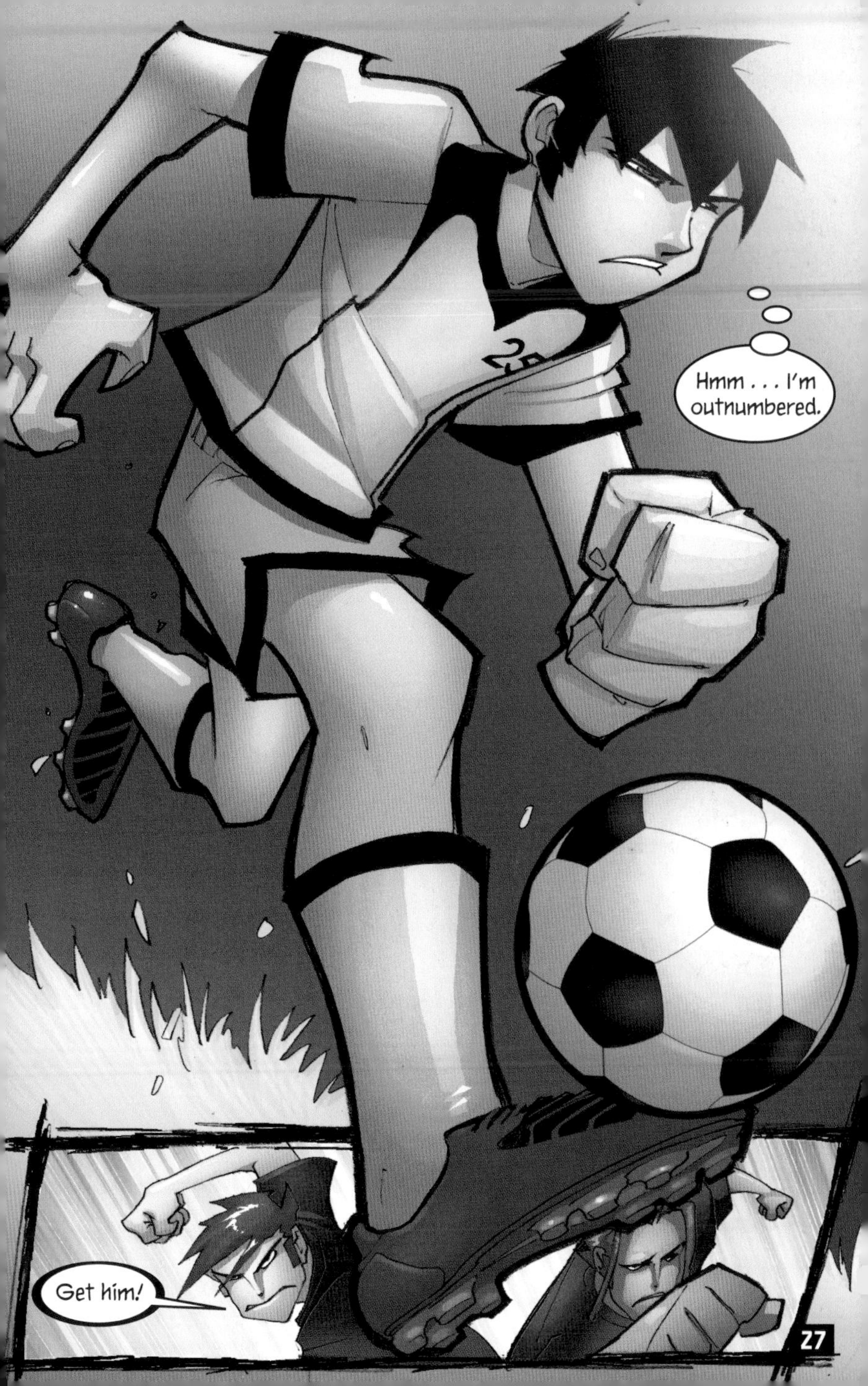
Hmm . . . I'm outnumbered.
Get him!

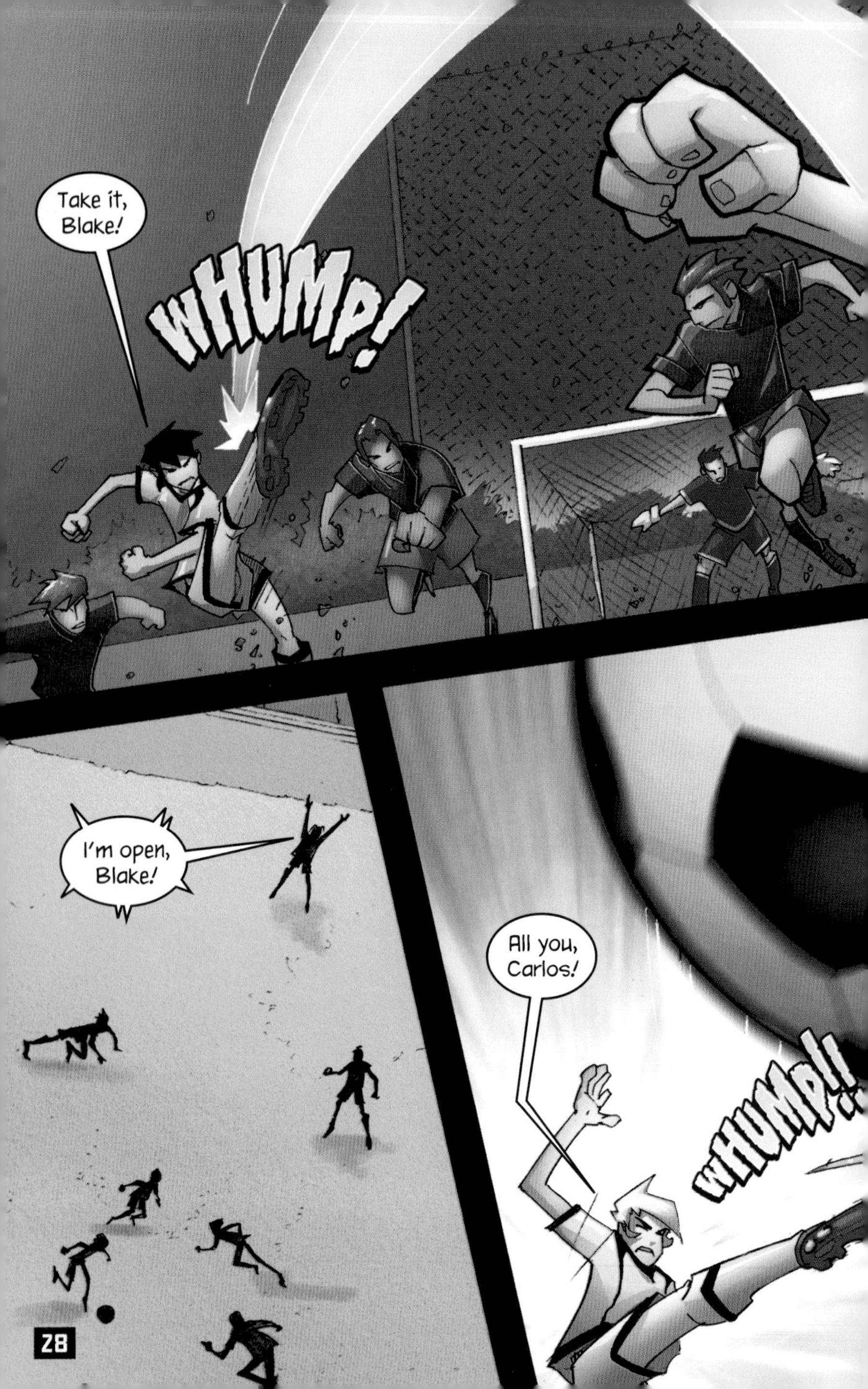
Take it, Blake!
wHUMP!
I'm open, Blake!
All you, Carlos!
wHUMP!!

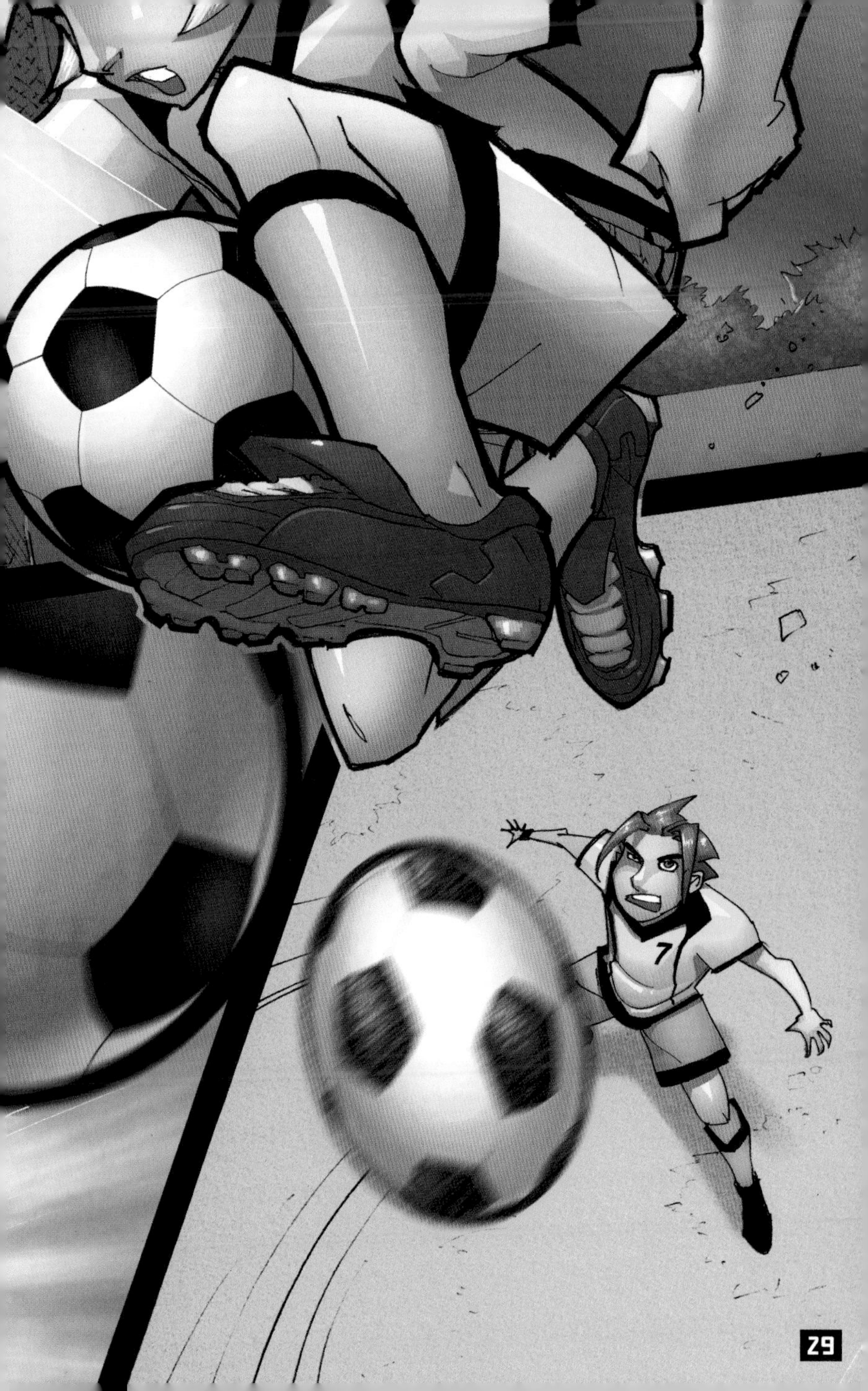

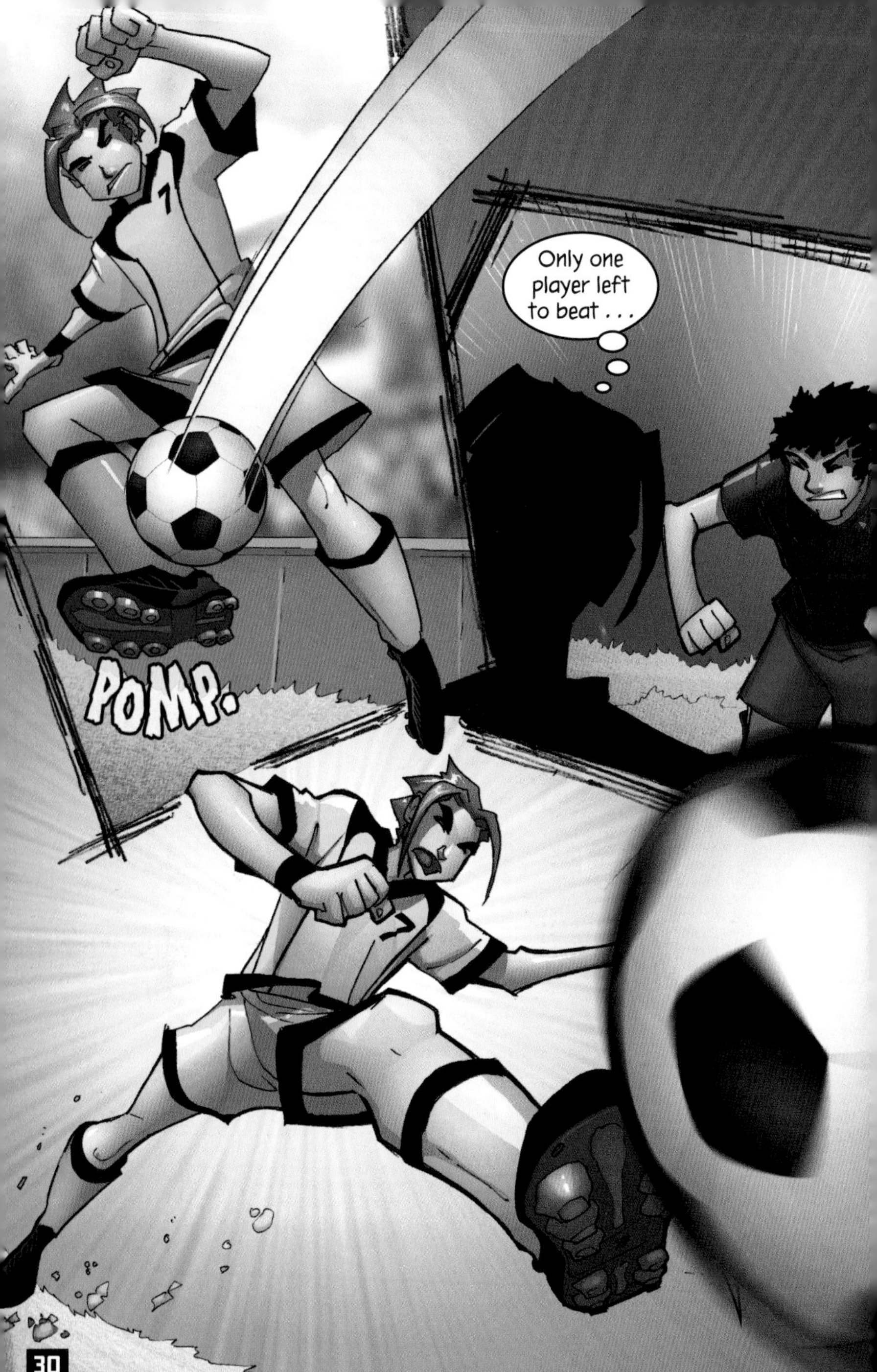
Only one player left to beat . . .
POMP.

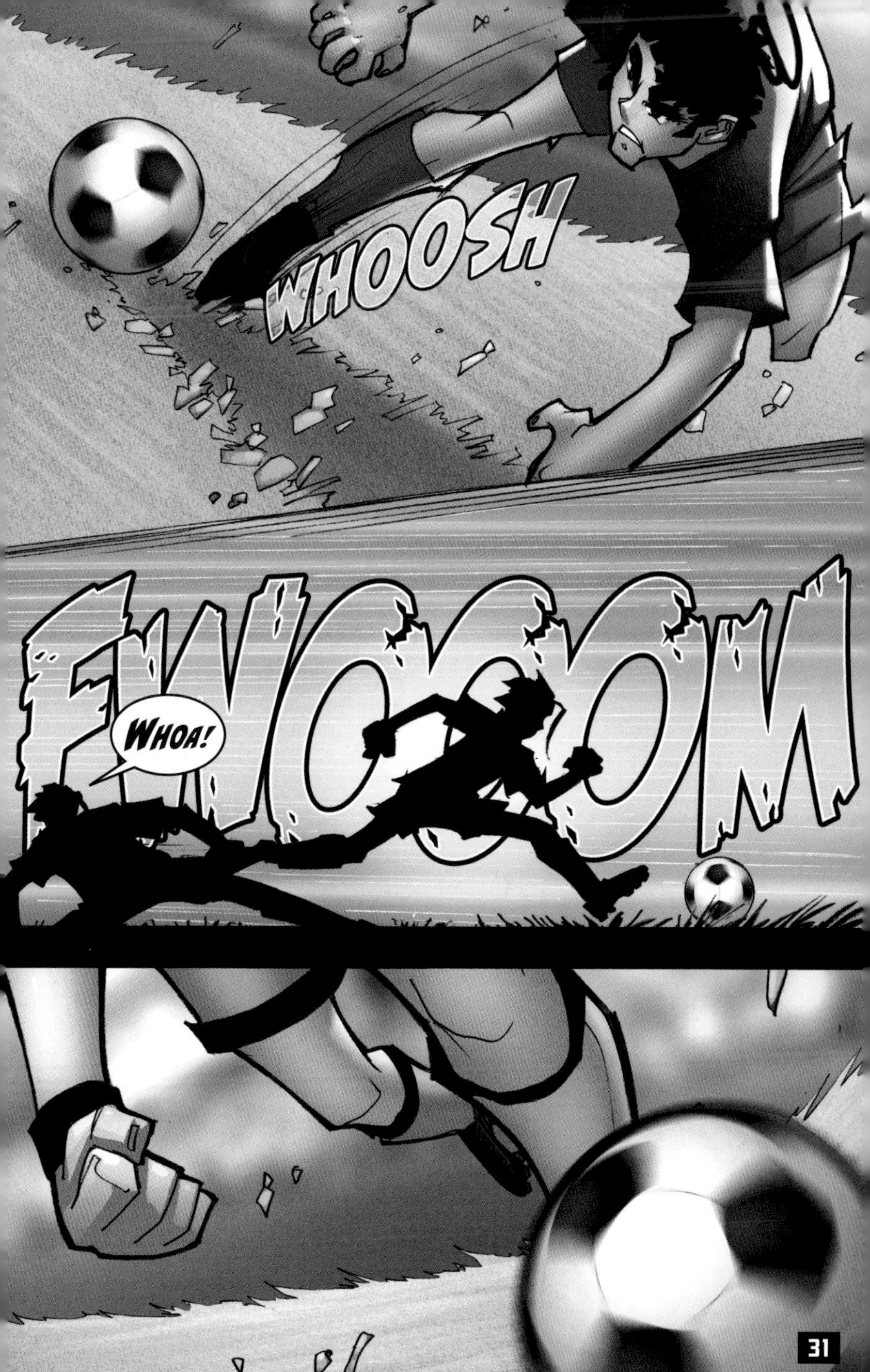
WHOOSH
FWOOOM
WHOA!

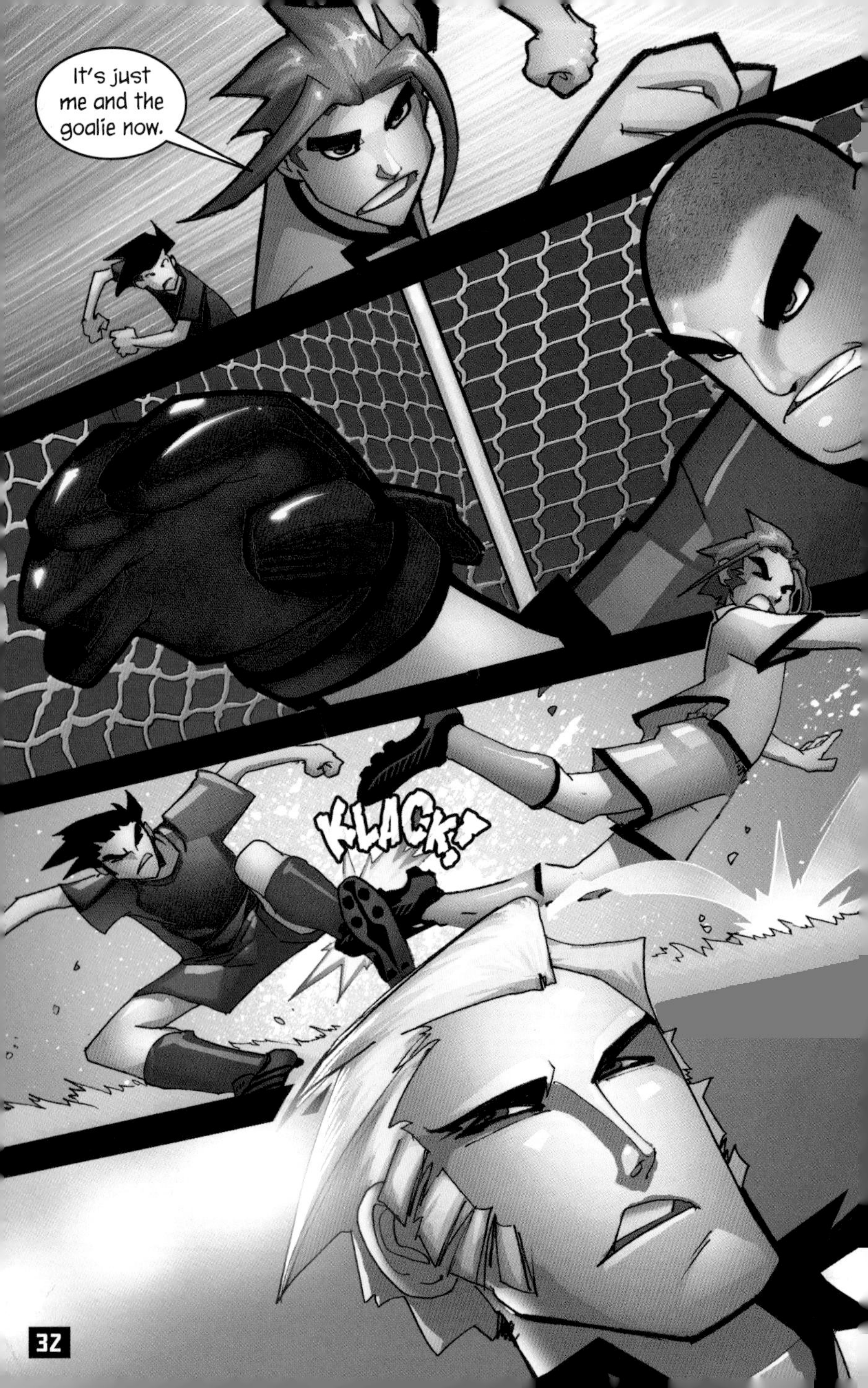

It's just me and the goalie now.
KLACK!

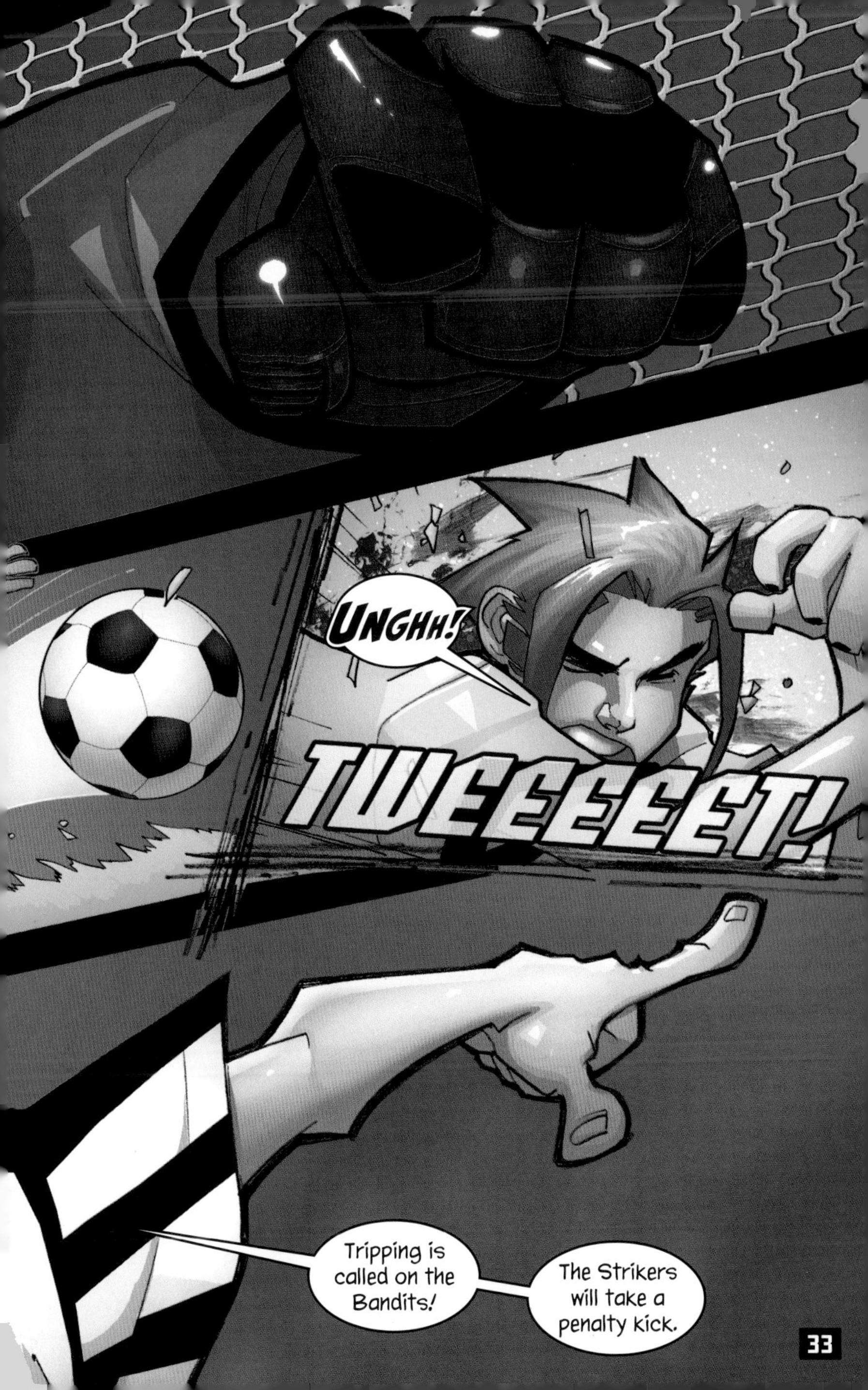
UNGHH!
TWEEEEET!
Tripping is called on the Bandits!
The Strikers will take a penalty kick.

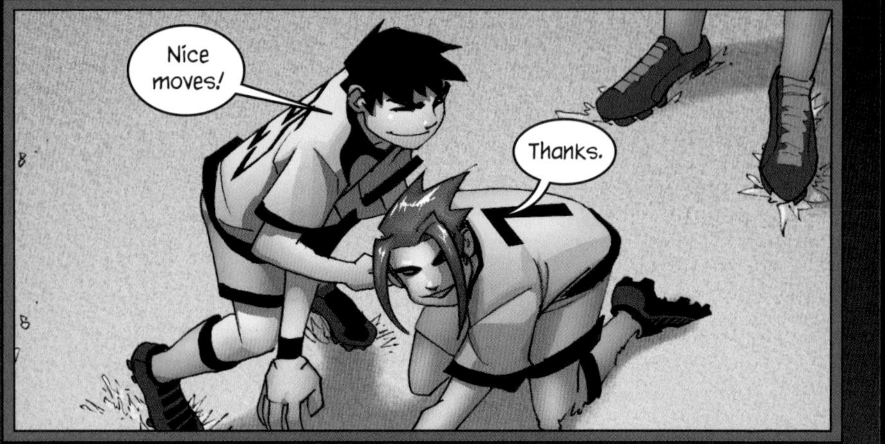
Nice moves!
Thanks.

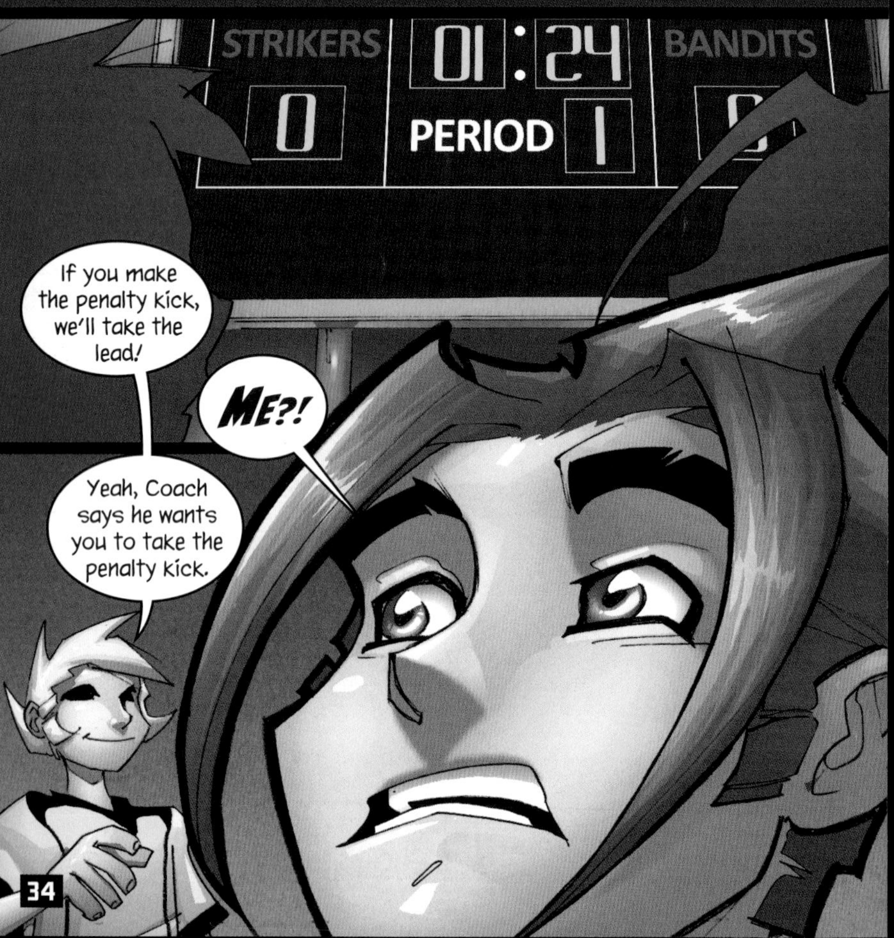
STRIKERS
01 : 24
BANDITS
0
PERIOD 1
If you make the penalty kick, we'll take the lead!
ME?!
Yeah, Coach says he wants you to take the penalty kick.

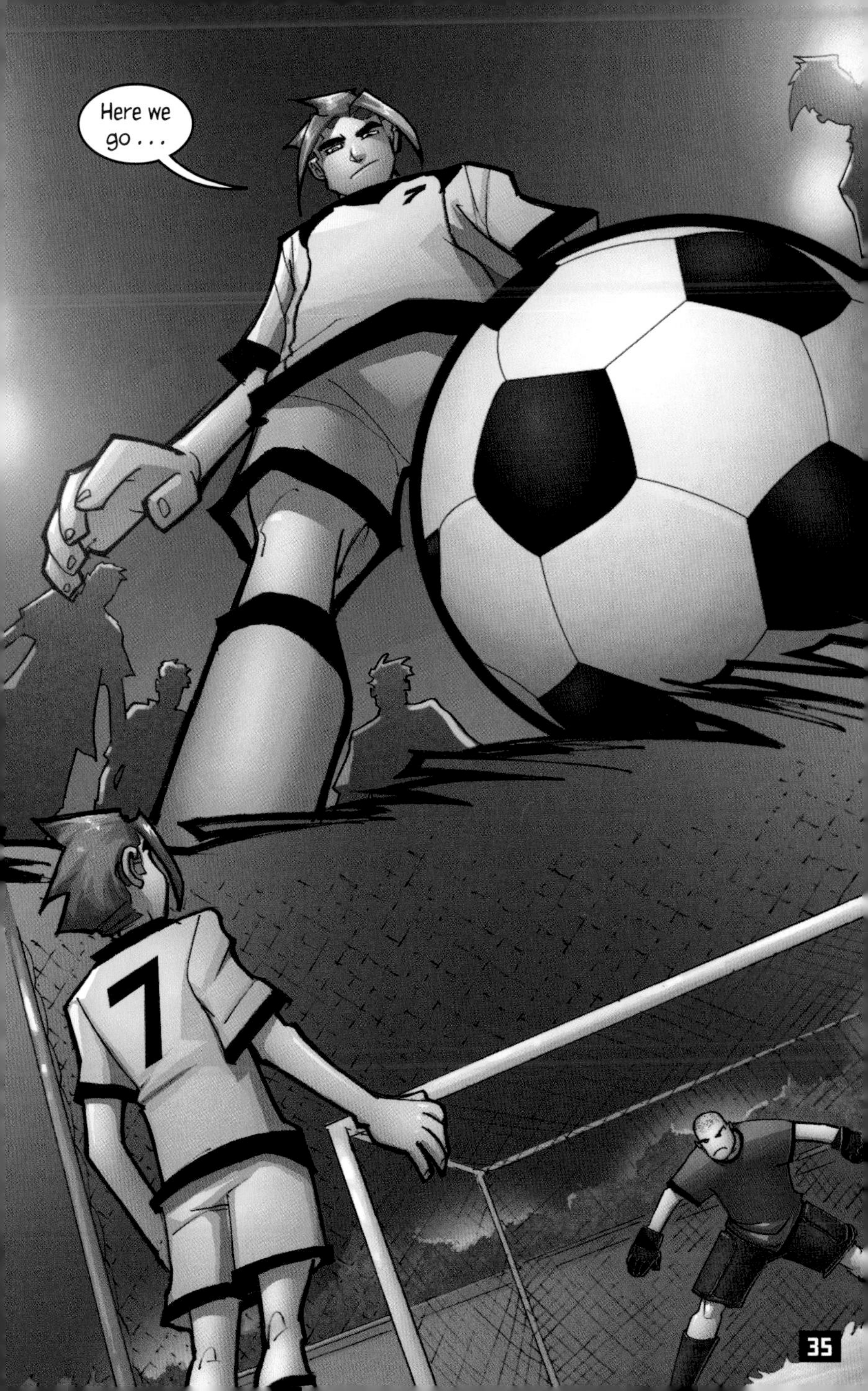
Here we go . . .

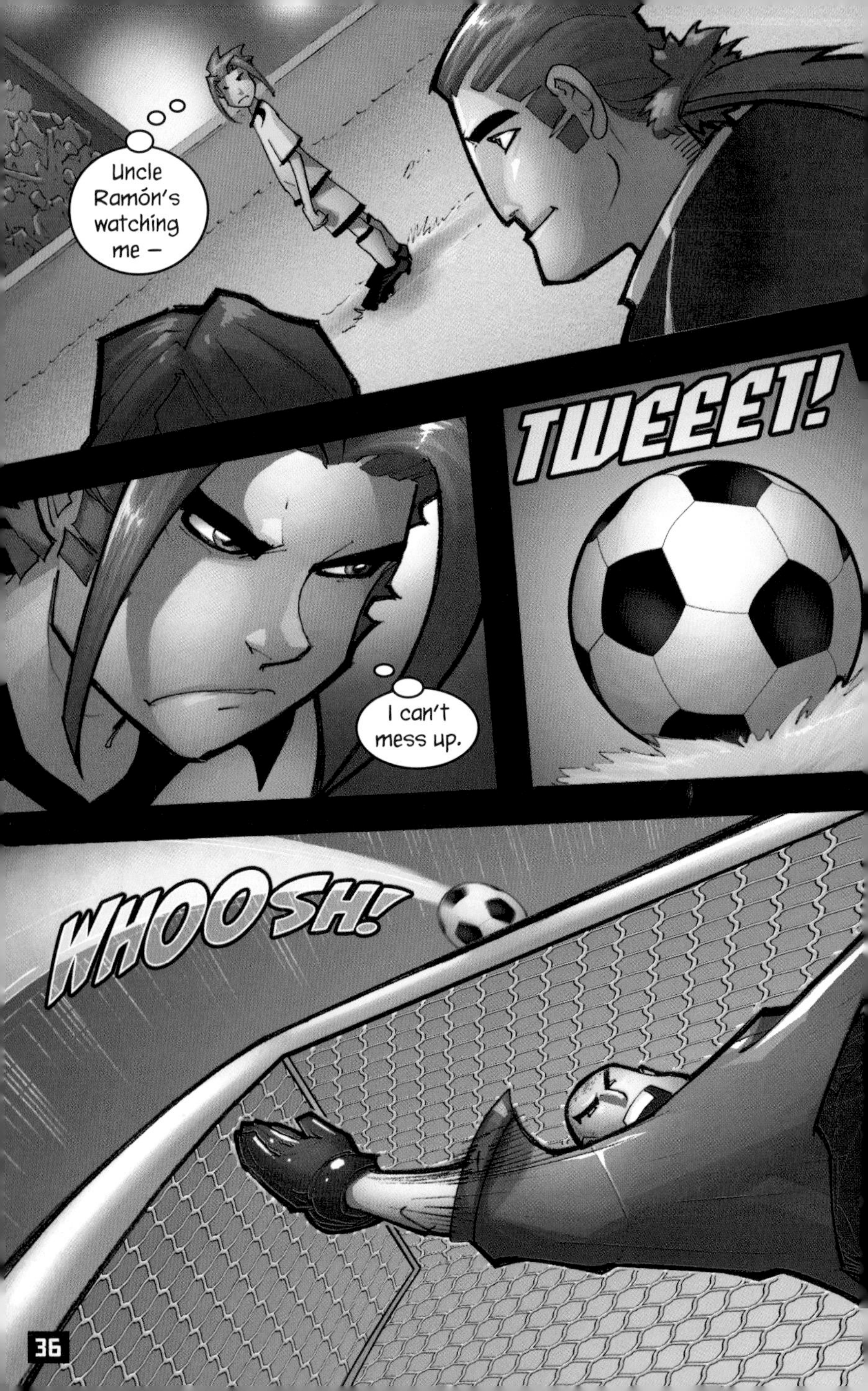
Uncle Ramón's watching me –
I can't mess up.
TWEEET!
WHOOSH!

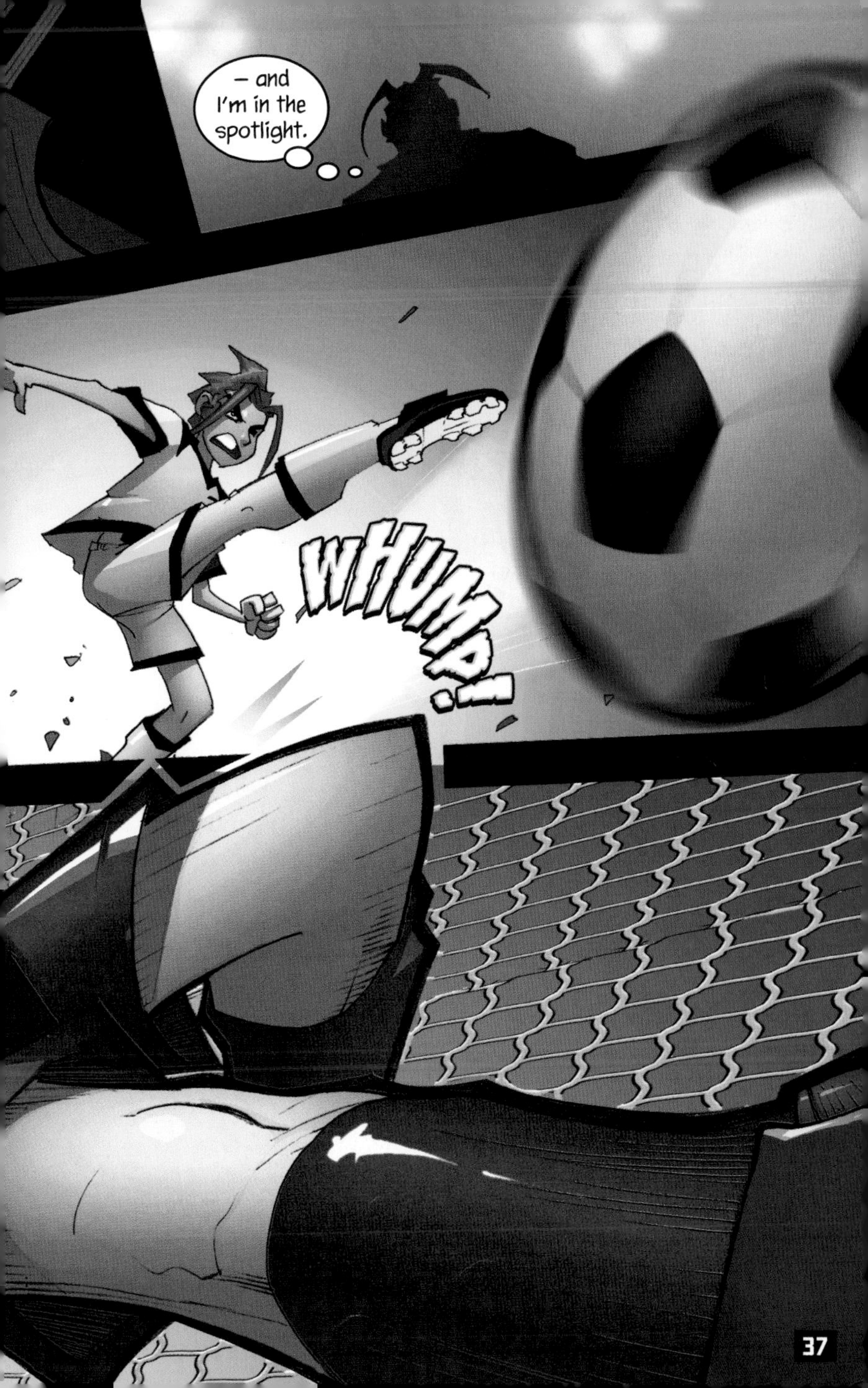
– and I'm in the spotlight.
WHUMP!!

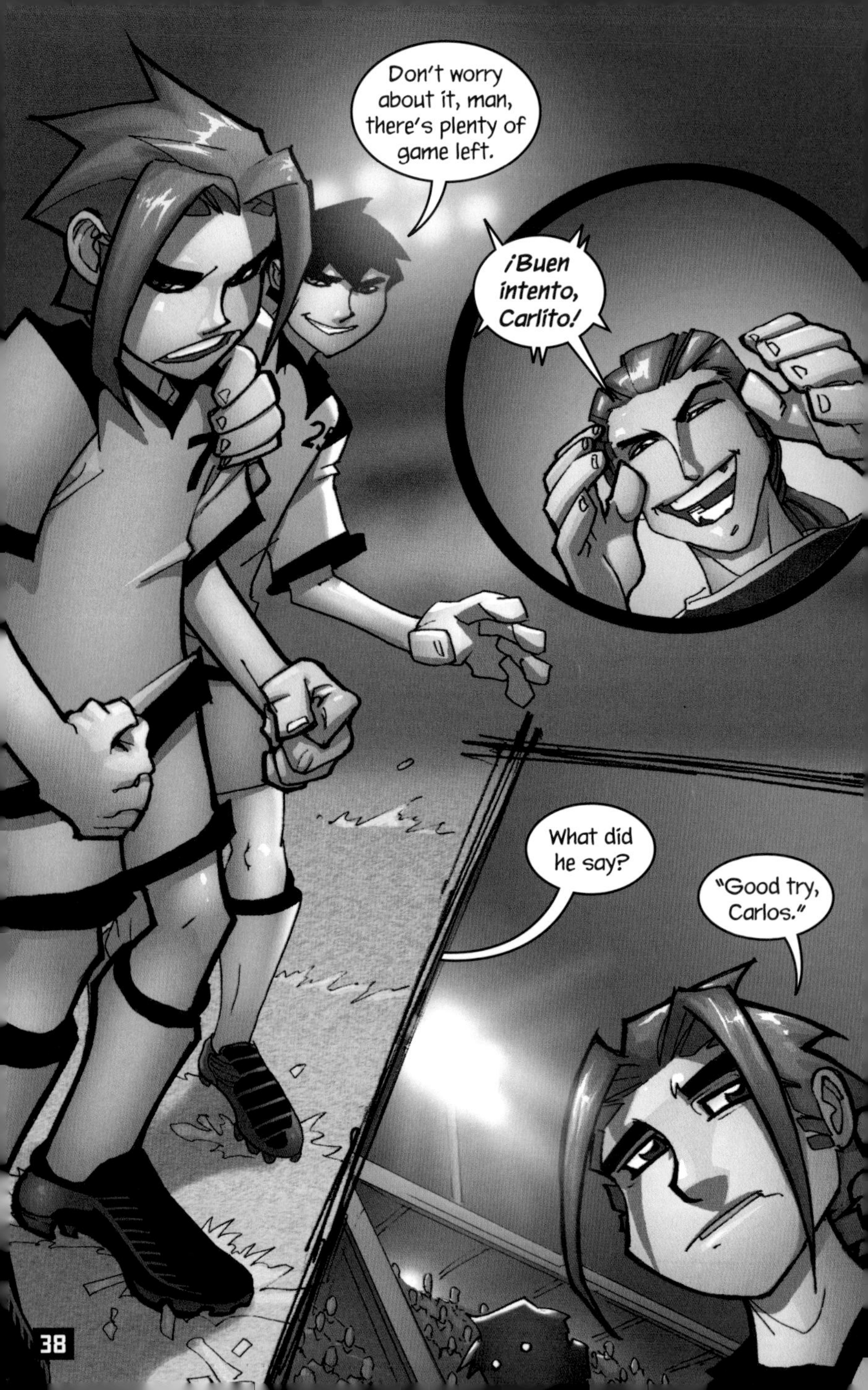
Don't worry about it, man, there's plenty of game left.
¡Buen intento, Carlito!
What did he say?
"Good try, Carlos."

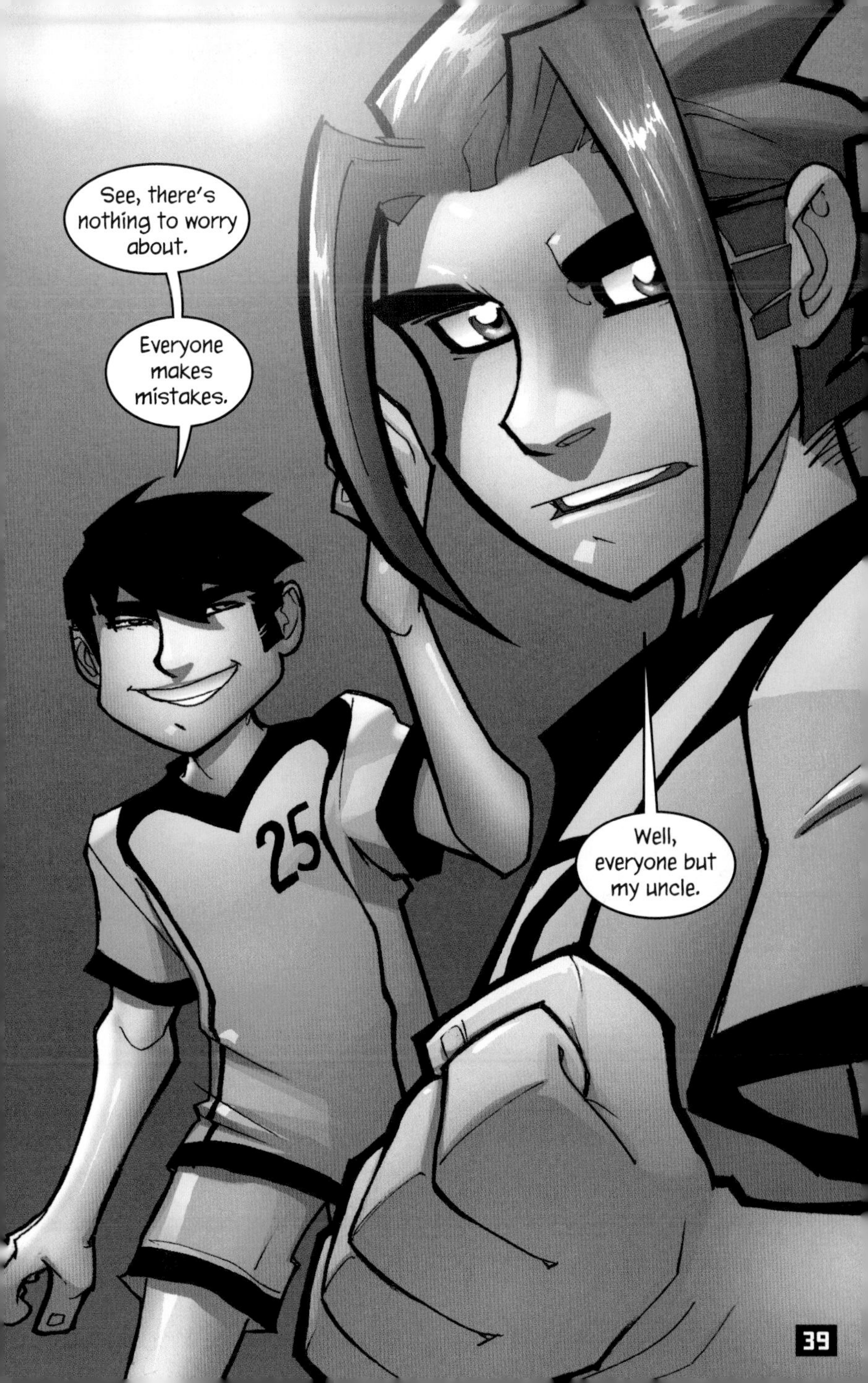
See, there's nothing to worry about.
Everyone makes mistakes.
Well, everyone but my uncle.
25

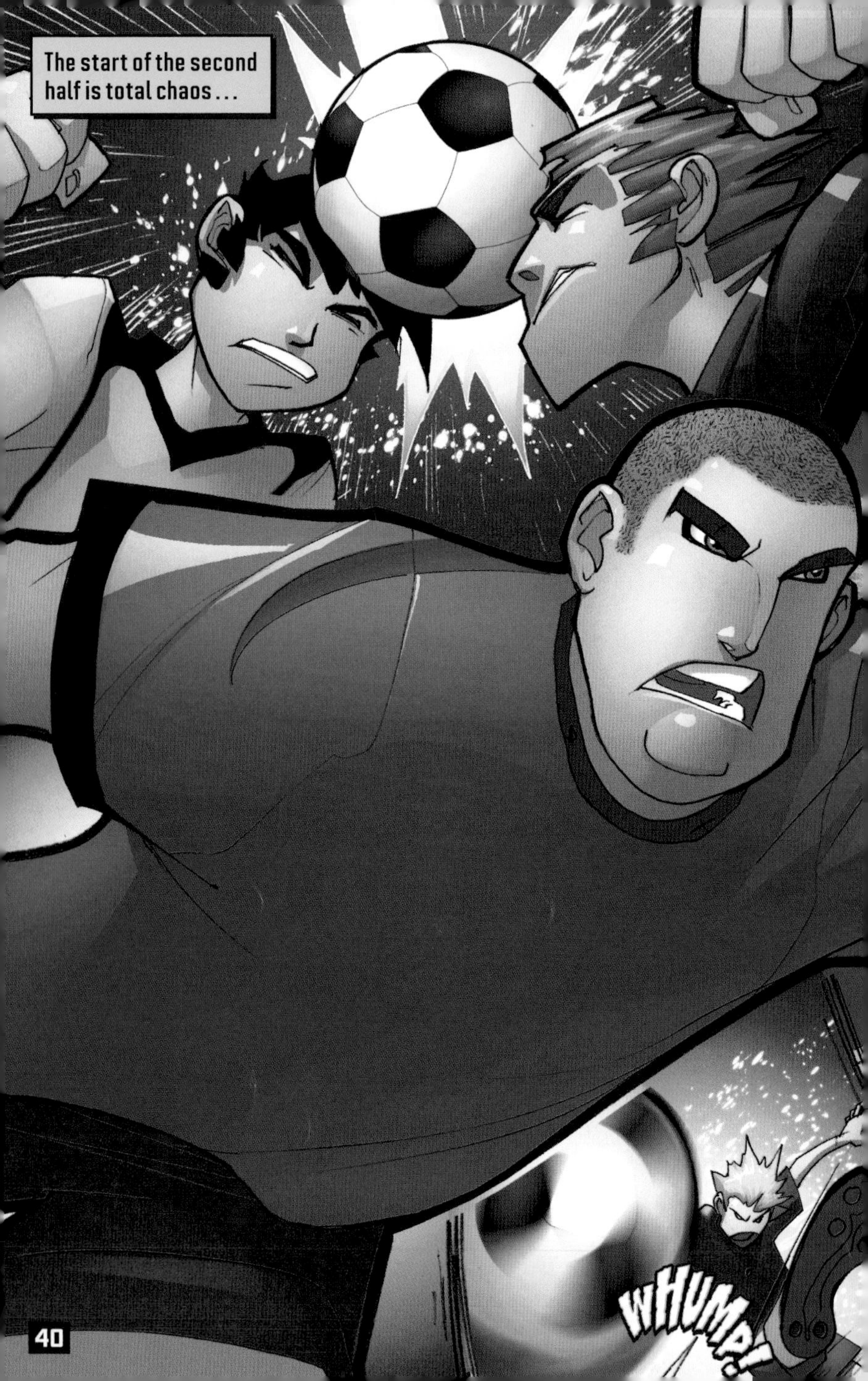
The start of the second half is total chaos . . .
WHUMP!

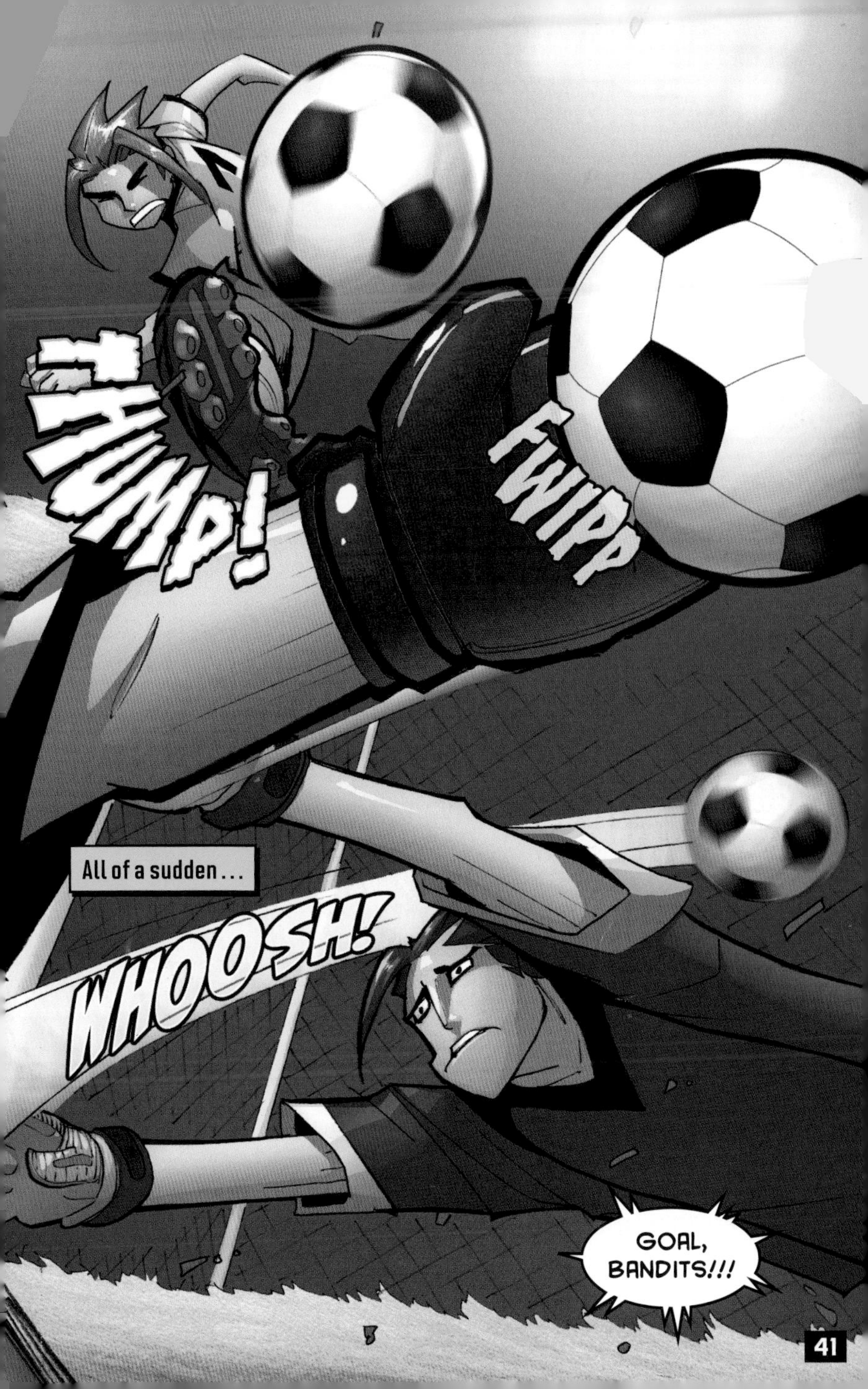

THUMP!
FWIPP
All of a sudden . . .
WHOOSH!
GOAL, BANDITS!!!

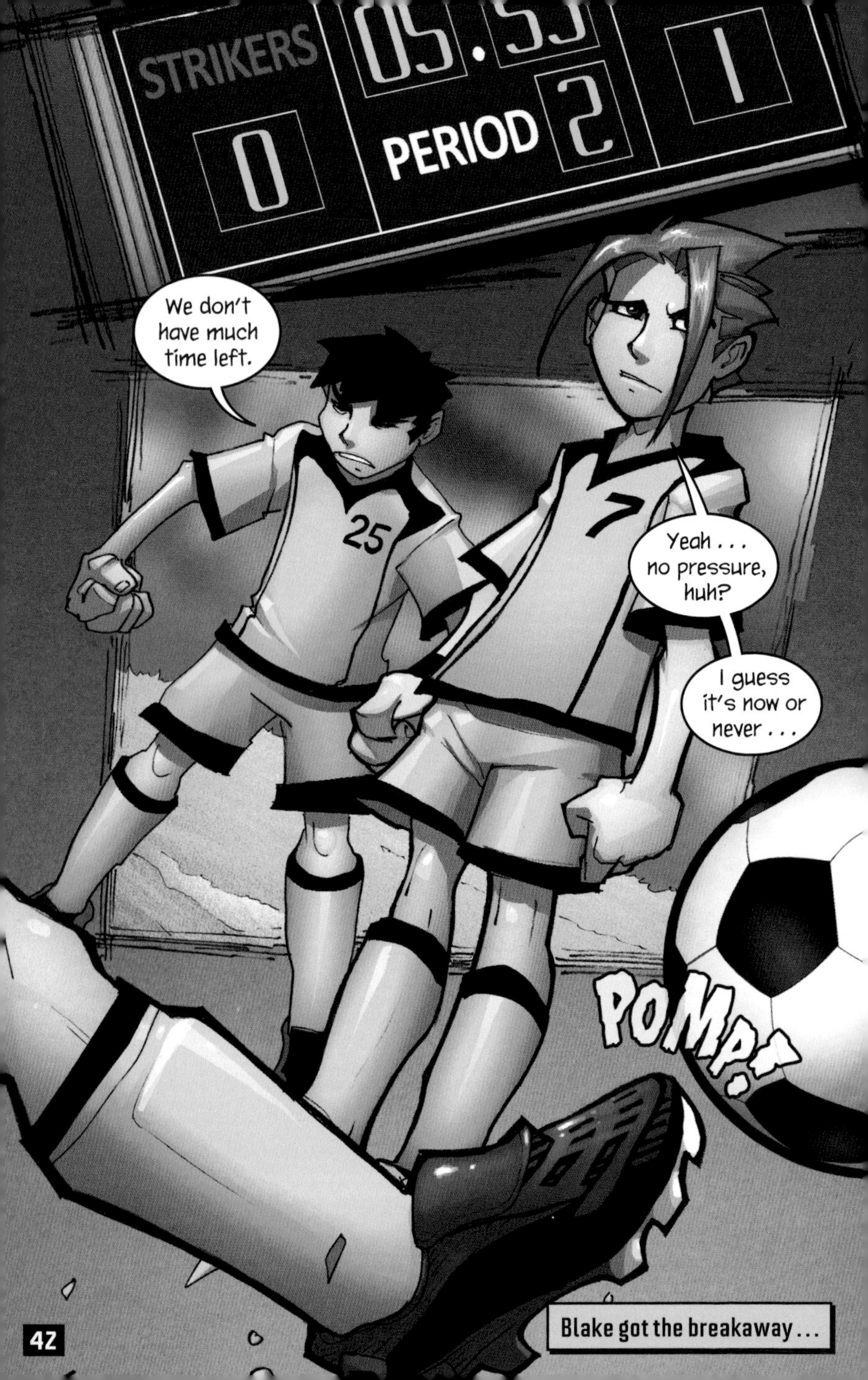
STRIKERS
05.55
1
0
PERIOD 2
We don't have much time left.
25
7
Yeah . . . no pressure, huh?
I guess it's now or never . . .
POMP!
Blake got the breakaway . . .

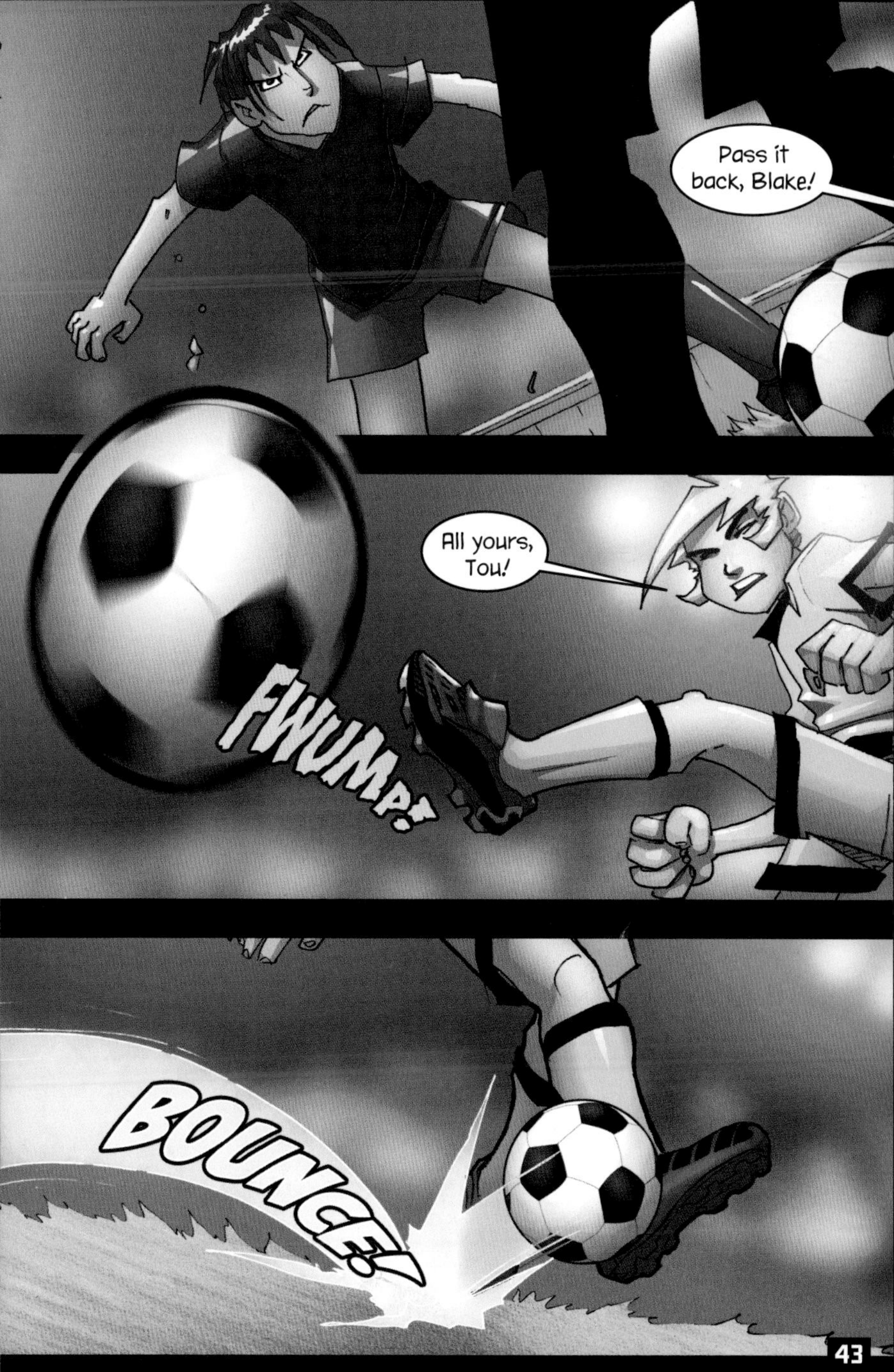
Pass it back, Blake!
All yours, Tou!
FWUMP!
BOUNCE!

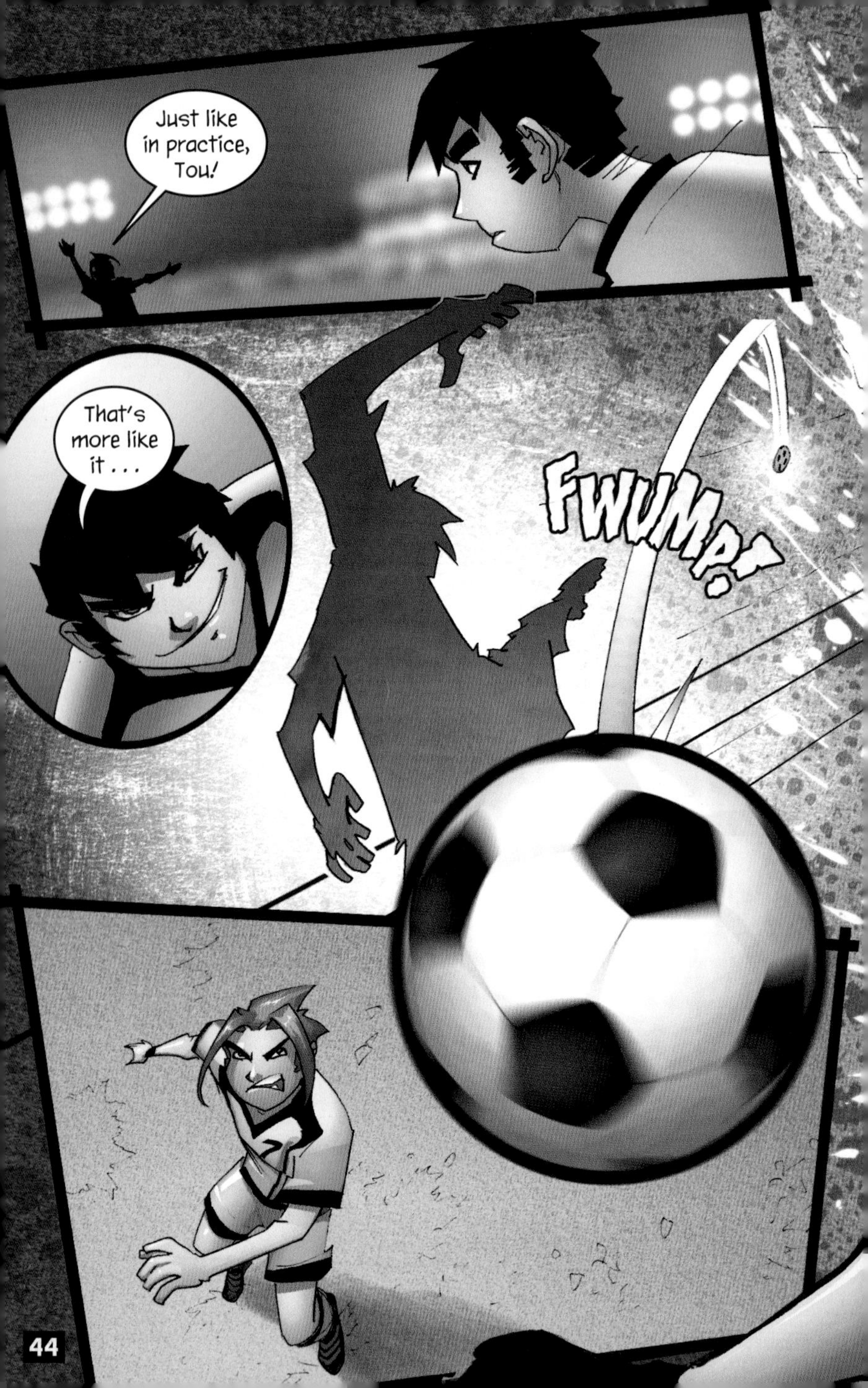
Just like in practice, Tou!
That's more like it . . .
FWUMP!

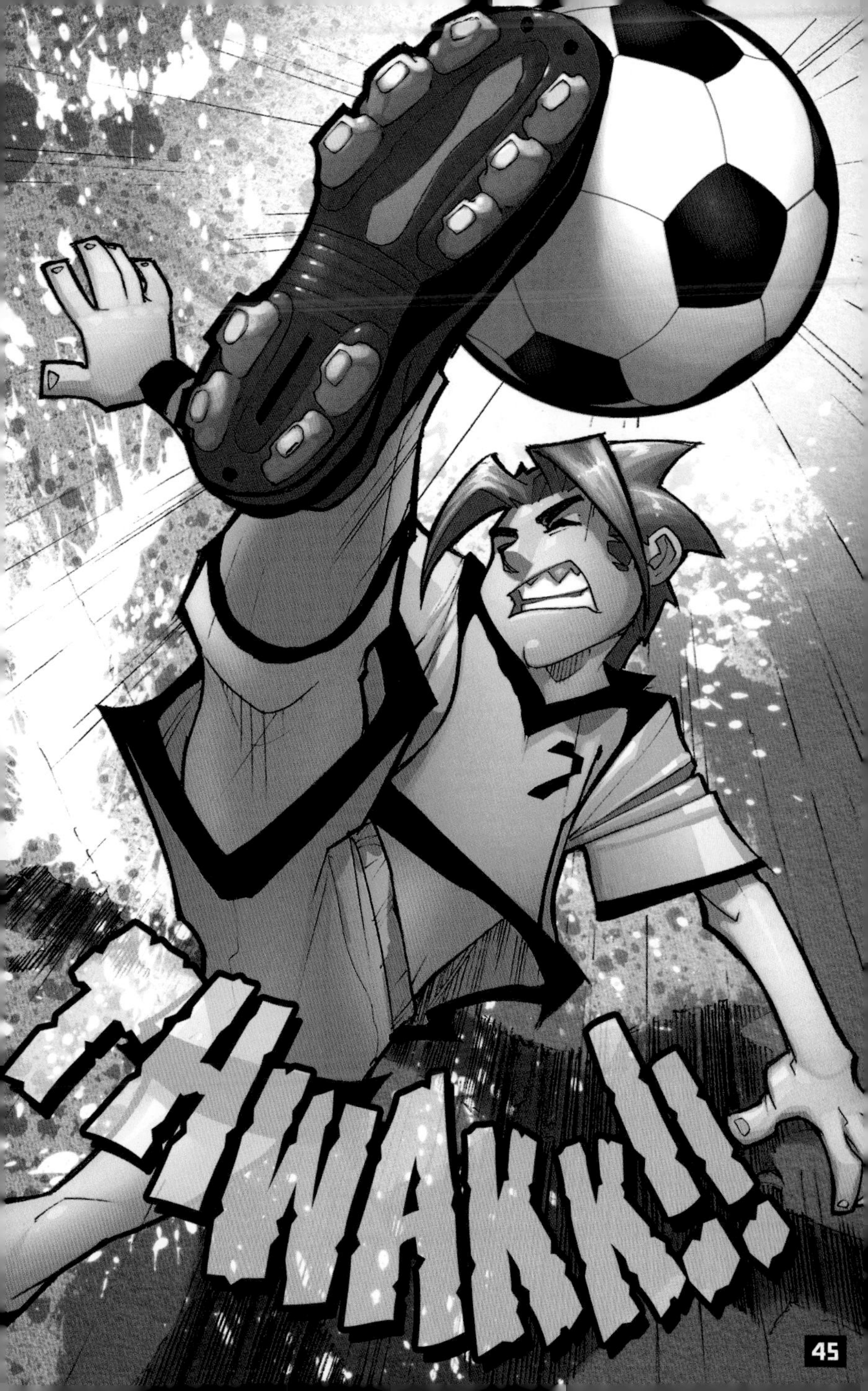
THWAKK!!

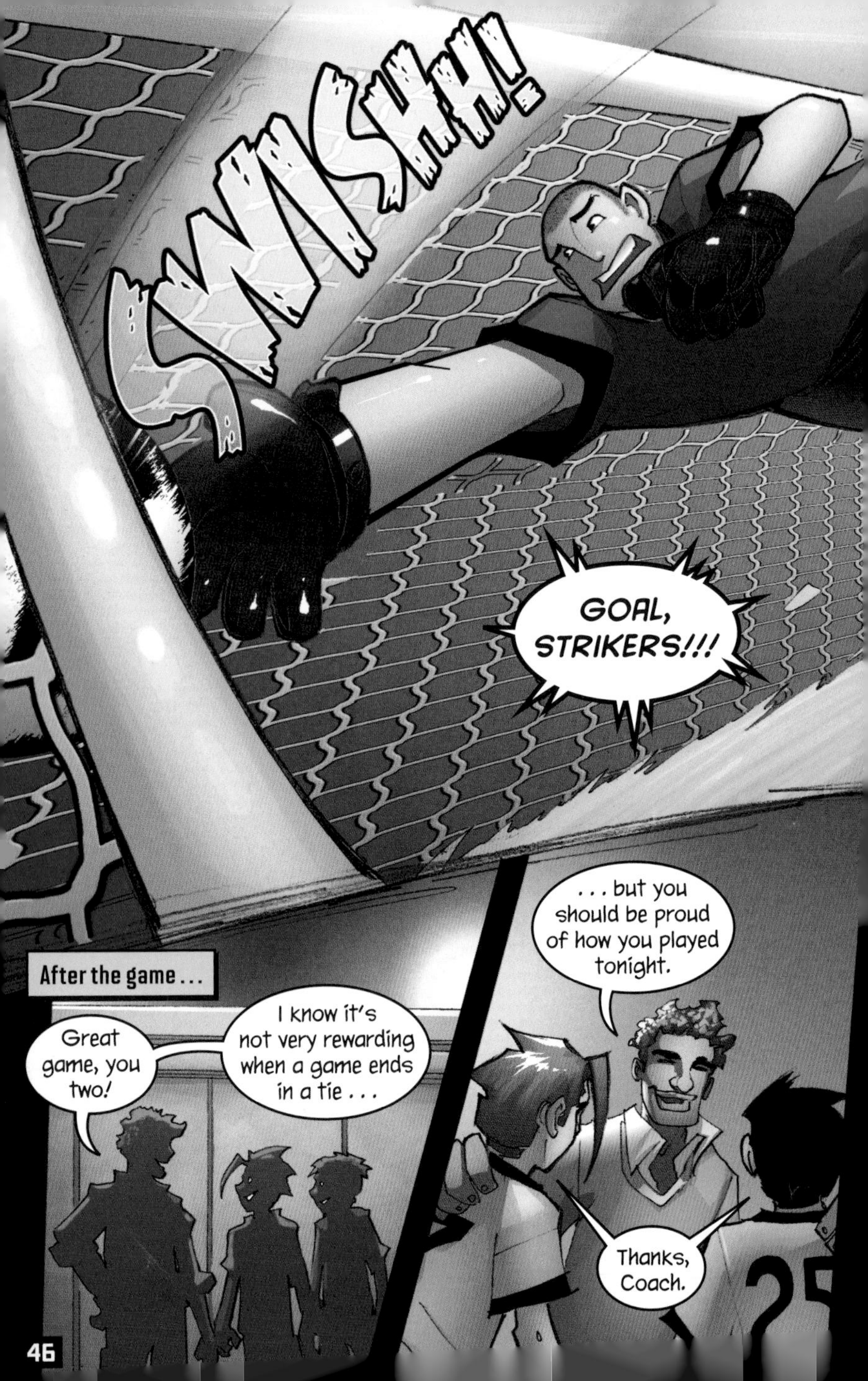
SWISHH!
GOAL, STRIKERS!!!
After the game . . .
Great game, you two!
I know it's not very rewarding when a game ends in a tie . . .
. . . but you should be proud of how you played tonight.
Thanks, Coach.

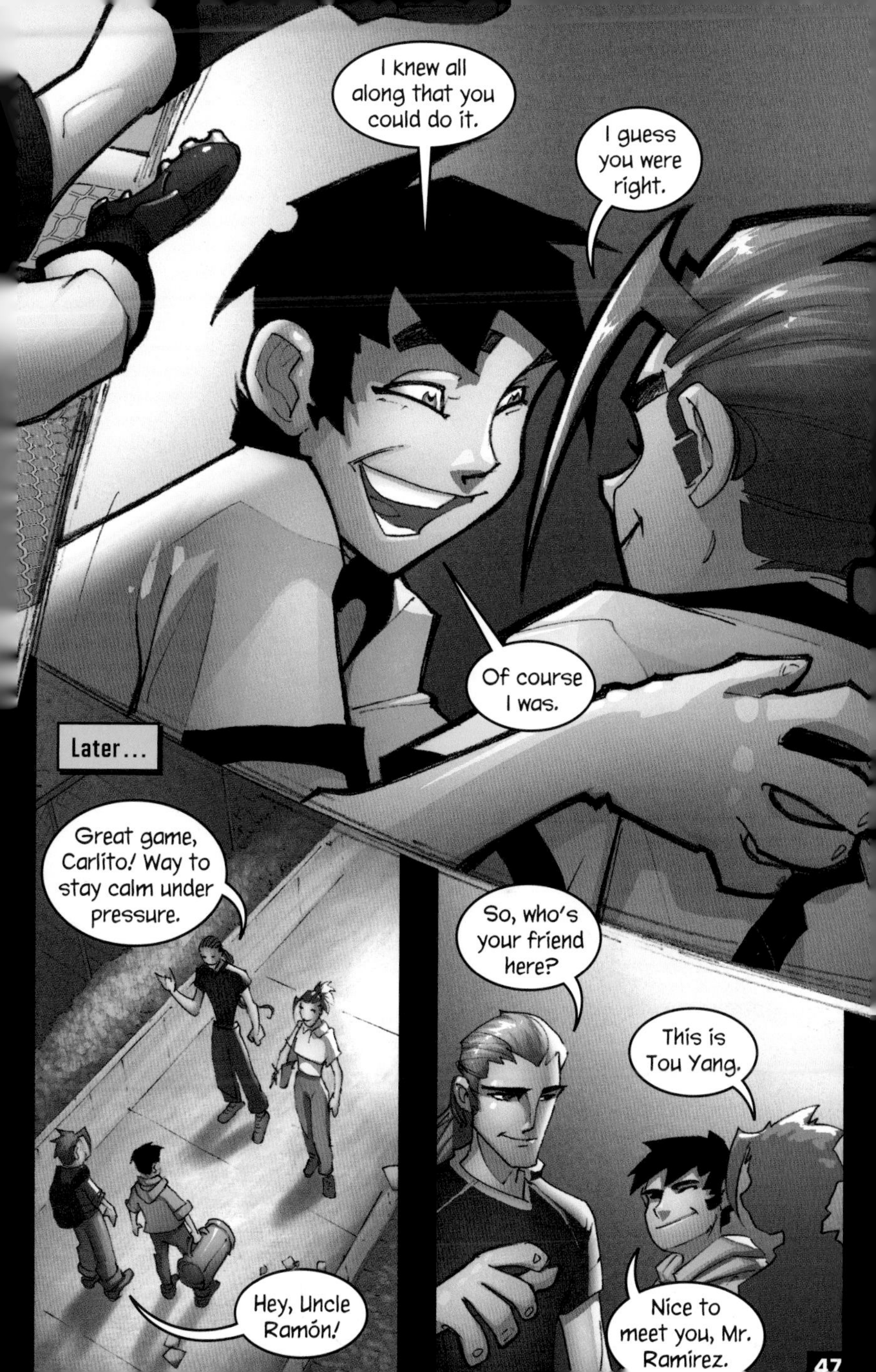

I knew all along that you could do it.
I guess you were right.
Of course I was.
Later...
Great game, Carlito! Way to stay calm under pressure.
Hey, Uncle Ramón!
So, who's your friend here?
This is Tou Yang.
Nice to meet you, Mr. Ramirez.

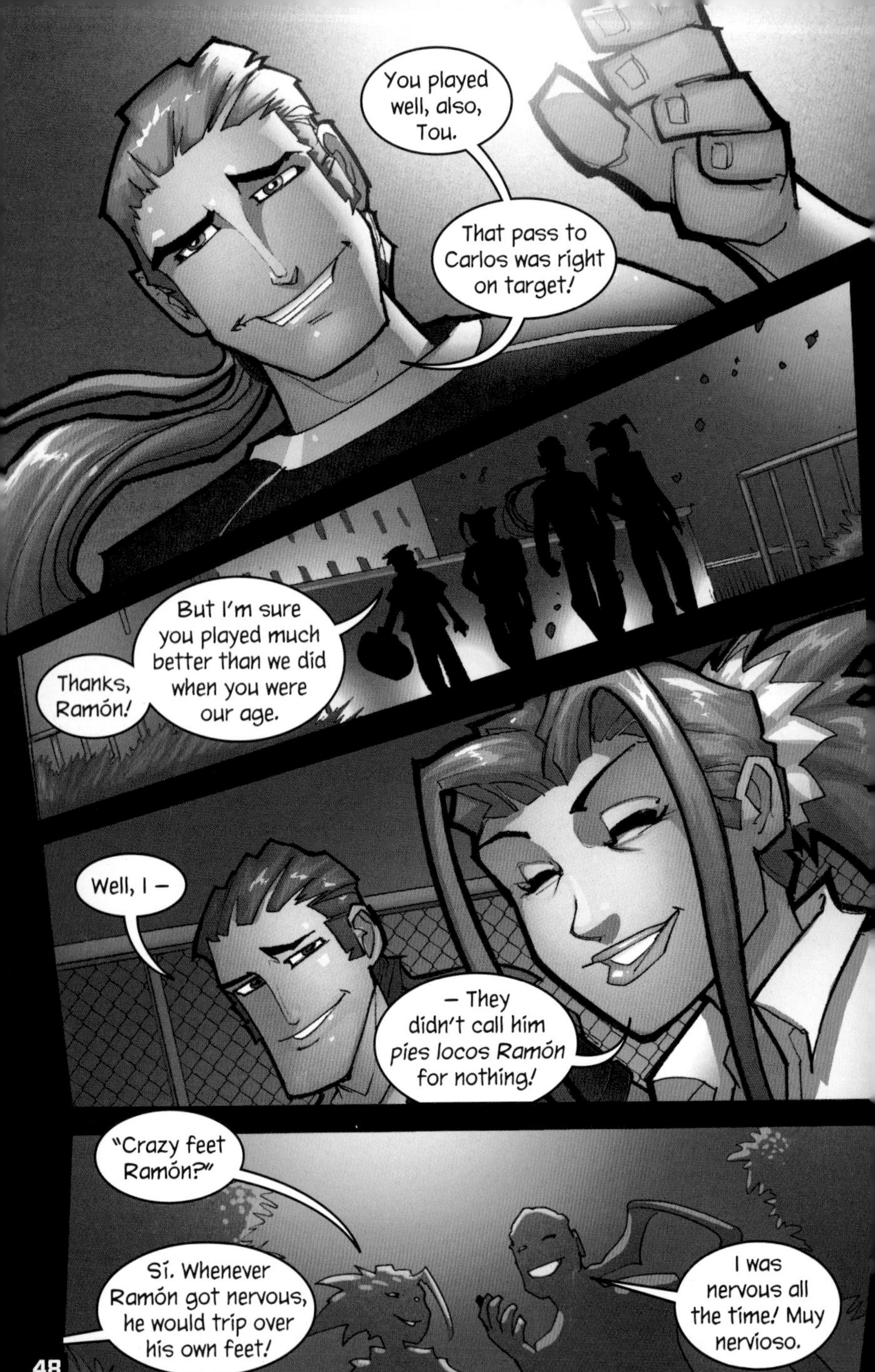
You played well, also, Tou.
That pass to Carlos was right on target!
Thanks, Ramón!
But I'm sure you played much better than we did when you were our age.
Well, I —
— They didn't call him *pies locos Ramón* for nothing!
"Crazy feet Ramón?"
Sí. Whenever Ramón got nervous, he would trip over his own feet!
I was nervous all the time! Muy nervioso.

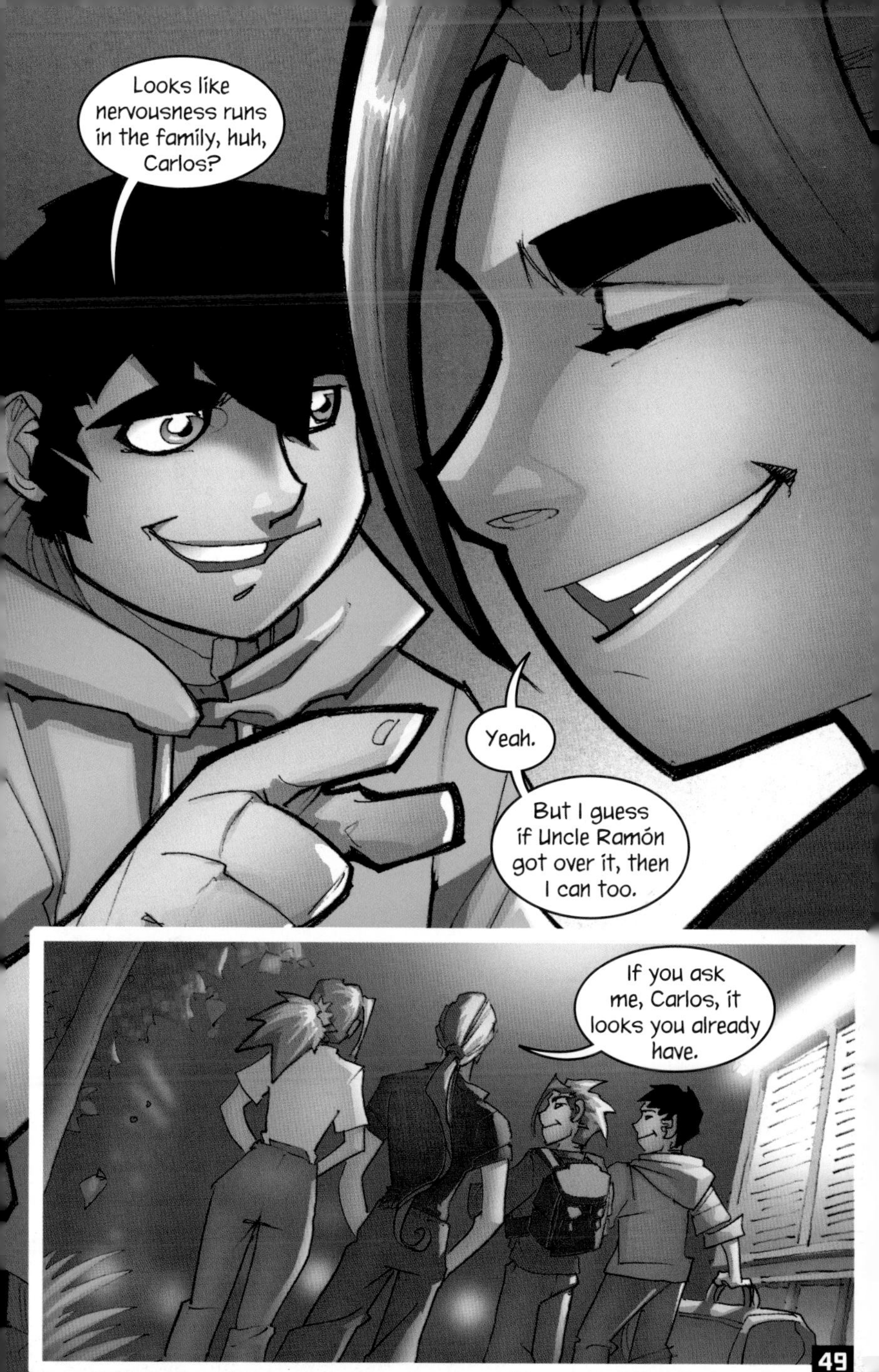
Looks like nervousness runs in the family, huh, Carlos?
Yeah.
But I guess if Uncle Ramón got over it, then I can too.
If you ask me, Carlos, it looks you already have.

SPORTS ZONE

POSTGAME RECAP

SOC
SOCCER

PNT
PAINTBALL

FBL
FOOTBALL

BSL
BASEBALL

BBL
BASKETBALL

HKY

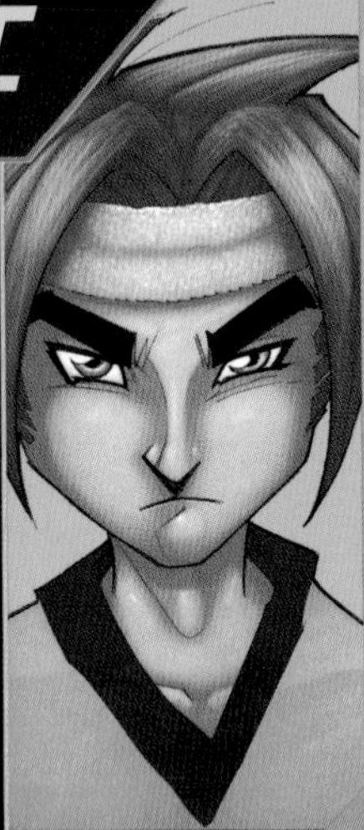

RAMIREZ

STRIKERS

SOCCER STAR STEPS UP AND SHINES IN THE SPOTLIGHT

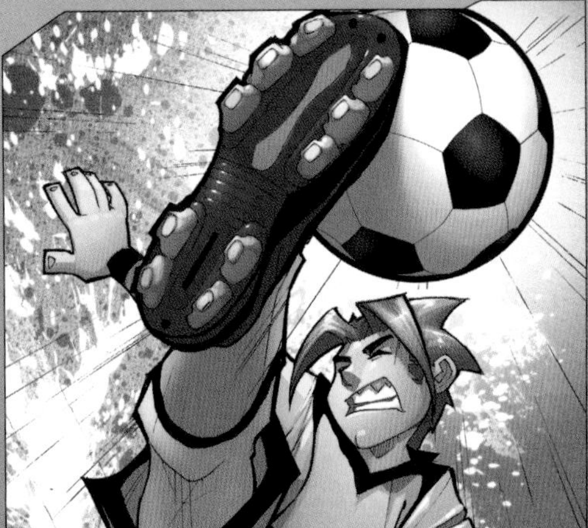

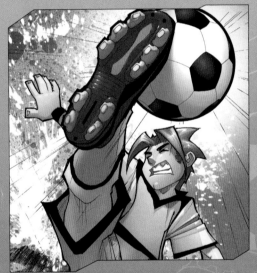

BY THE NUMBERS

FINAL SCORE:
STRIKERS: 1
BANDITS: 1

GOALS:
RAMIREZ: 1
ROGERS: 1

STORY: Carlos Ramirez overcame his fears to lead the Strikers to a tie against the ultra-talented Bandits. Any doubts about Carlos's ability to perform under pressure were silenced with the resounding thud of his game-tying goal — and he even did it by way of an incredible bicycle kick! If today's game is any indication, the Strikers have a big season ahead of them.

Sports Illustrated KIDS

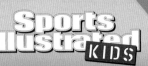

UP NEXT: SI KIDS INFO CENTER

SZ **POSTGAME EXTRA**

WHERE **YOU** ANALYZE THE GAME!

BLZ vs BNS
3·1
TGR vs RO:
33·3,
EAG vs BA:
14·7
SPA vs WI:
4·3
BAN vs RO:
21·15
RZR vs LIG
4·3
BLZ o BN!
7-7

Soccer fans were served up a real surprise when the Strikers tied the Bandits in a heated matchup. Let's go into the stands and ask some fans about the day's events...

DISCUSSION QUESTION 1

What do you think about games that end in a tie? Does there always have to be a winner? Why or why not?

DISCUSSION QUESTION 2

Which character in this book is your favorite — Tou, Carlos, Uncle Ramón, or Coach Daniels? Why?

WRITING PROMPT 1

Carlos is nervous about playing in front of his uncle. When was the last time that you were nervous? What happened? Write about a nervous experience.

WRITING PROMPT 2

Carlos has a talented uncle. Do you have any skilled relatives? What have they done that is impressive? Write about your special family members and friends.

(uh-SIST)—one or two passes that directly lead to a goal

(BYE-si-kuhl KIK)—when a player kicks the ball over his head in mid-air with his back facing the ground

(di-FENS-muhn)—players whose main task is to stop the opposing team from scoring

(DRAW)—a game that ends with a tied score

(FOR-wurdz)—players who are tasked with scoring most of their team's goals. They play in front of the rest of the team.

(HED-ur)—a kick or pass done with a player's head

(MID-feel-durz)—players who link together the offense and defense of a team. They play behind forwards.

(PEN-uhl-tee KIK)—a kick taken from the penalty spot against the opposing goalie

(STRYK-er)—a team's most talented forward who plays near the center of the field

EATORS

BLAKE A. HOENA › *Author*

Blake A. Hoena grew up in central Wisconsin, where he wrote stories about trolls lumbering around in the woods behind his parent's house. Later, he moved to Minnesota to pursue a Masters in Creative Writing from Minnesota State University, Mankato. Since graduating, Blake has written more than thirty books for children, including graphic novel retellings of *The Legend of Sleepy Hollow* and the Perseus and Medusa myth, as well as *Kickoff Blitz.*

GERARDO SANDOVAL › *Illustrator*

Gerardo Sandoval is a professional comic book illustrator from Mexico. He has worked on many well-known comics including the Tomb Raider books from Top Cow Productions. He has also worked on designs for posters and card sets.

BENNY FUENTES › *Colorist*

Benny Fuentes lives in Villahermosa, Tabasco in Mexico, where it's just as hot as the sauce is. He studied graphic design in college, but now he works as a full-time colorist in the comic book industry for companies like Marvel, DC Comics, and Top Cow Productions. He shares his home with two crazy cats, Chelo and Kitty, who act like they own the place.

Sports Illustrated KIDS GRAPHIC NOVELS

QUICK COMIC

CHESTER COYOTE and CORA RAMIREZ IN:

PAINTBALL PUNK

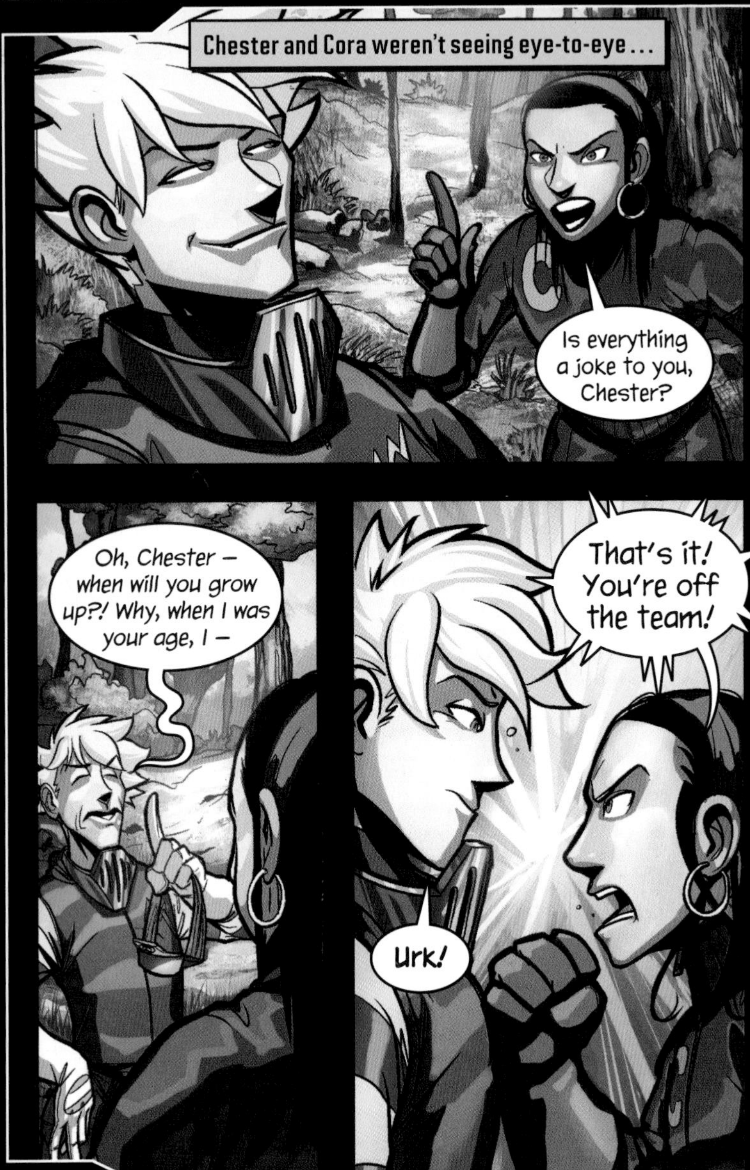
Chester and Cora weren't seeing eye-to-eye . . .
Is everything a joke to you, Chester?
Oh, Chester — when will you grow up?! Why, when I was your age, I —
That's it! You're off the team!
Urk!

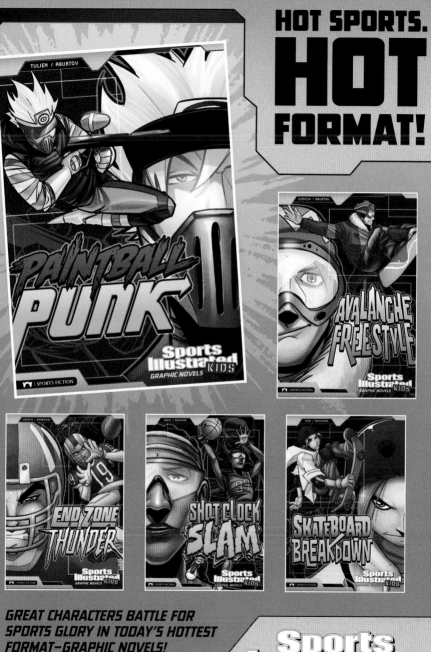

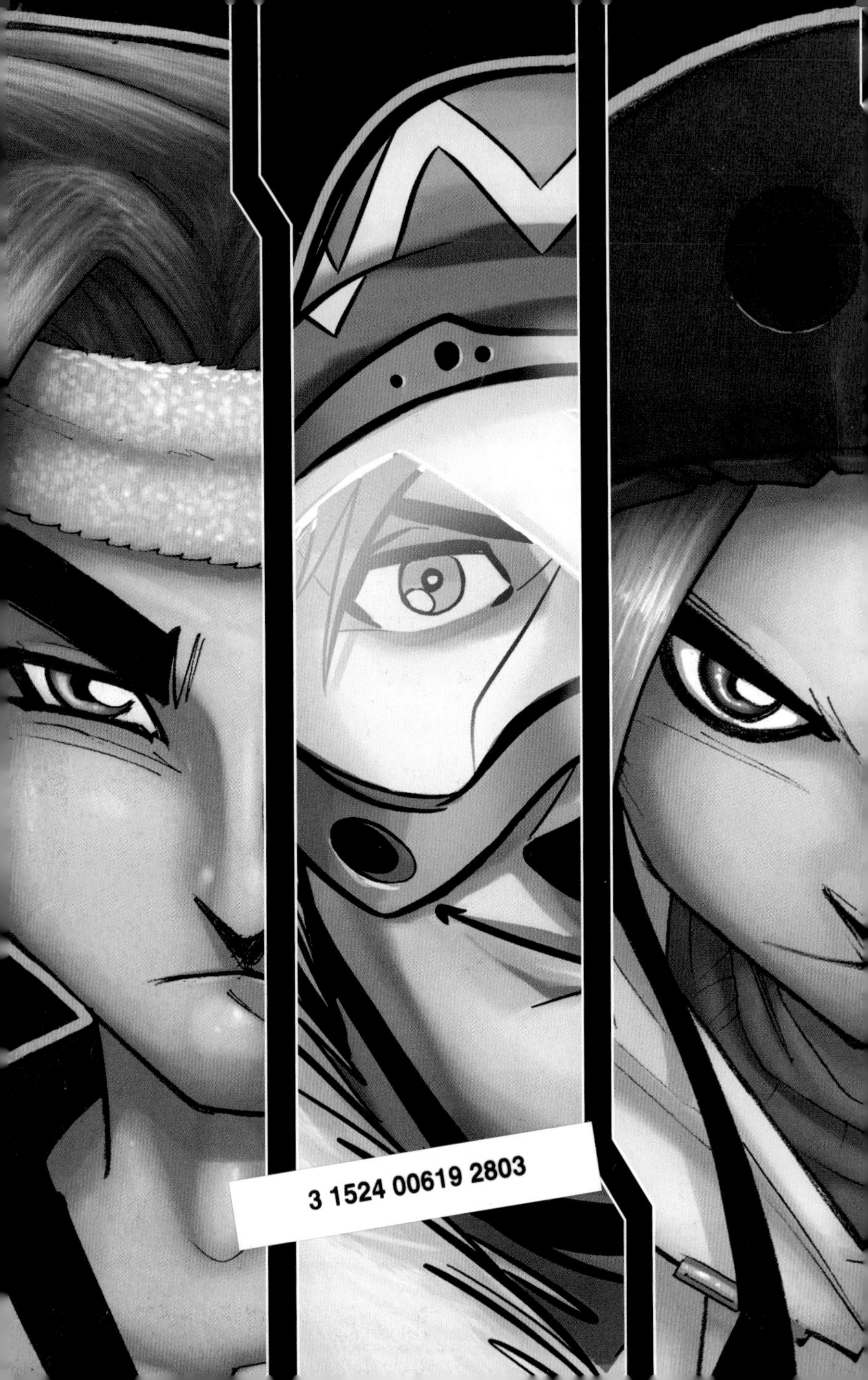